WENDELL BERRY

T0191302

Also by Wendell Berry

FICTION
Andy Catlett
Hannah Coulter
Fidelity
Jayber Crow
The Memory of Old Jack
Nathan Coulter
A Place on Earth
Remembering
That Distant Land
Watch With Me
The Wild Birds

POETRY
The Broken Ground
Clearing
Collected Poems: 1957–1982
The Country of Marriage
Entries
Farming: A Hand Book
Findings
Openings
A Part
Sabbaths
Sayings and Doings
The Selected Poems of Wendell Berry (1998)
A Timbered Choir
The Wheel

ESSAYS
The Way of Ignorance
Another Turn of the Crank
The Art of the Commonplace
Citizenship Papers
A Continuous Harmony
The Gift of Good Land
Harlan Hubbard: Life and Work
The Hidden Wound
Home Economics
Life Is a Miracle
Long-Legged House
Recollected Essays: 1965–1980
Sex, Economy, Freedom and Community
Standing by Words
The Unforeseen Wilderness
The Unsettling of America
What Are People For?

A World Lost

WENDELL BERRY

A World Lost

a novel

COUNTERPOINT

BERKELEY

This book is a work of fiction. Nothing is in it that has
not been imagined.

Lines from "Don't Get Around Much Anymore" © 1944
Robbins Music Corporation. Used with permission.

Library of Congress Cataloging-in-Publication Data
Berry, Wendell, 1934-
A World Lost : a novel / Wendell Berry
p. cm.
ISBN-13: 978-1-58243-418-6
ISBN-10: 1-58243-418-2
1. Port William (Ky. : Imaginary place)—Fiction.
2. Country life—Fiction. 3. Kentucky—Fiction.
4. Death—Fiction I. Title.
ps3552.e75w67 2008
813'.54—dc22   2007044428

Book design by David Bullen
Printed in the United States of America

Counterpoint
2560 Ninth Street
Suite 318
Berkeley, CA 94710
www.counterpointpress.com

10 9

The dead rise and walk about
The timeless fields of thought

A World Lost

1

It was early July, bright and hot; I was staying with my grandmother and grandfather Catlett. My brother, Henry — who might have been there with me; we often made our family visits together — was at home at our house down at Hargrave. For several good and selfish reasons, I did not regret his absence. When we were apart we did not fight, we did not have to decide who would get what we both wanted, we did not have to trump up disagreements just to keep from agreeing. The day would come when there would be harmony between us and we would be allies, but we had many a trifle to quarrel over before then.

Uncle Andrew, who often ate dinner at Grandma Catlett's, was at work up on the river at Stoneport, as he had been for a week already. He had refused to take me with him. This was in the summer of 1944, when I was nine, nearly ten. The war had made building materials scarce. My father and Uncle Andrew, along with Uncle Andrew's buddies, Yeager Stump and Buster Simms, had bought the buildings of a defunct lead mine at Stoneport with the idea of salvaging the lumber and sheet metal to build some barns. The work was heavy and somewhat dangerous; it was going to take a long time. I could not go because I was too short in the push-up. I felt a little blemished by Uncle Andrew's refusal, and I missed him. Now and again I experienced the tremor of my belief that the adventure of Stoneport had been subtracted from me forever. But I was reconciled. As I was well aware, there were advantages to my solitude.

No day at Grandma and Grandpa's was ever the same as any other, but there were certain usages that I tried to follow, especially when I was there alone. That afternoon, as soon as I could escape attention, I knew I would go across the field to Fred Brightleaf's. Fred and I would catch Rufus Brightleaf's past-work old draft horse, Prince, and ride him over to the pond for a swim. And after supper, when Grandma and Grandpa would be content just to sit on the front porch in the dark, and you could feel the place growing lonesome for other times, I would drift away down to the little house beside the woods where Dick Watson and Aunt Sarah Jane lived. While the light drained from the sky and night fell I would sit with Dick on the rock steps in front of the door and listen to him tell of the horses and mules and foxhounds he remembered, while Aunt Sarah Jane spoke biblical admonitions from the lamplit room behind us; to her, Judgment Day was as much a matter of fact, and as visible, as the Fourth of July.

I was comfortable with the two of them as I was with nobody else, and I am unsure why. It was not because, as a white child, I was free or privileged with them, for they expected and sometimes required decent behavior of me, like the other grown-ups I knew. They had not many possessions, and the simplicity in that may have appealed to me; they did not spend much time in anxiety about *things*. They had too a quietness that was not passive but profound. Dick especially had the gift of meditativeness. Because he was getting old, what he meditated on was the past. In his talk he dreamed us back into the presence of a supreme work mule named Fanny, a preeminent foxhound by the name of Strive, a long-running and uncatchable fox.

There had been, anyhow, only three of us at the table in Grandma's kitchen that noon: Grandma and Grandpa and me. After dinner, Grandpa got up and went straight back to the barn. I sat on at the table, liking the stillness that filled the old house at such times. The whole world seemed stopped and quiet, as if the sun stood still a moment between its rising up and its going down; you could hear the emptiness of the rooms where nobody was. And then Grandma set the dishpan on the stove and started scraping up our dishes. She had her mind on her work then, and I headed for the door.

"Where are you off to, Andy, old traveler?"

"Just out," I said.

She let me go without even a warning. The good old kitchen sounds were rising up around her. As I went out across the porch I heard her start humming "Rock of Ages." When she was young she had been a good singer, but her voice was cracked now and she could not sustain the notes.

I went down through the field we still called the Orchard, though only one old apple tree was left, and then into the Lower Field, across the part of it that had been cut for hay, and then followed the dusty two-track road around the edge of a field of corn. I saw the groundhog that I planned to shoot as soon as I got old enough to have a .22 rifle. Grandma always put dinner on the table at eleven-thirty, and so it was still close to noon. My shadow was almost underfoot, and I amused myself by stepping on its head as I went along. I was wearing a coarse-woven straw hat that Uncle Andrew had bought for me, calling it "a two-gallon hat, plenty good for a half-pint." The sun shone through holes in the brim in a few places, making little stars in the shadow. I walked fast, telling myself the story of myself: "The boy is walking across the farm. He is by himself. Nobody knows where he is going. It is a pretty day."

On the far side of the cornfield I went through a gate into the creek road and then through another gate into the lane that went up to the Brightleafs' house. There was a row of tall Lombardy poplars that somebody had planted along the little stream that flowed from the Chatham Spring. When I got into the shadow of the first poplar I stopped and called, "Oh, Fred!"

Nobody answered. All around it was quiet. I walked the stepping-stones across the stream and went up to the house, knowing already that nobody was home but not wanting to believe it. I went all the way up to the yard fence and called again. It was a fact. Nobody was there, except for Jess Brightleaf's old bird dog, Fern, who had a litter of pups under the front porch, and Mrs. Brightleaf's old hens who looked at me from their dust holes under the snowball bush and did not get up. It was hot and sweaty, the kind of afternoon that makes you think of water.

Everybody was gone, and for a minute or two I felt disappointed and lonesome. But then the quiet changed, and I ceased to mind. All at once the countryside felt big and easy around me, and I was glad to be alone in it.

I looked at the sugar pear tree, but no pears were ripe yet, and I went on down to the spring. Some of the Chathams had lived there once and had left their name with the good vein of water that flowed from the bedrock at the foot of the hill. But the Chathams probably had not called it the Chatham Spring; probably they had called it after somebody who had been there before—maybe after an Indian, I thought. People named springs after other people, not themselves.

The Chatham Spring was cunningly walled and roofed with rock. There was a wooden door that you opened into a little room, moist and dark, where the vein flowed out of the hill into a pool deep enough for the Brightleafs to dip their buckets. The water flowed out of the pool under a large foot-worn rock that was the threshold of the door. The Brightleafs carried all their household water from the spring.

I opened the door. When my eyes had accepted the dimness I could see the water striders' feet dimpling the surface of the pool and a green frog on a glistening ledge just above the water. I fastened the door and lay down outside at the place I liked best to drink, which was just below the threshold stone where the water was flowing and yet so smooth that it held a piece of the sky in it as still and bright as a set in a ring. The water was so clear you could look down through the reflection of the sky or your face and see maybe a crawfish. I took my hat off and drank big swallows, relishing the coldness of the water and the taste it carried up from the deep rock and the darkness inside the hill. As I drank, the light lay warm on my back like a hand, and I could smell the mint that grew along the stream. When I had drunk all I could hold I put my nose into the water, and then my whole face.

The Chatham Spring had never been dry, not even in the terrible summers of 1908 and 1930 and 1936. People spoke of it as "an everlasting spring." There was a line of such springs lying across that part of the country, and all of them had been cared for a long time and bore the names of families: Chatham and Beechum and Branch and Bower and Coulter. There were days, I knew, when my Grandfather Catlett would ride horseback from one to the other, arriving at each one thirsty, to drink, savor, and reflect on the different tastes of the different waters, those thirsts and quenchings, tastes and differences being signs of something he profoundly knew. And I, as I drank and wetted my face, thought of the springs and of him, my mind leaning back out of the light and into time.

🦋

From the spring I went back to the creek road and across and through another gate and up the long slope of an unclipped pasture. I could see my grandfather's steers gone to shade in a grove of locust trees on up the creek. I walked a while through the ripened bluegrass stems and the clover and Queen Anne's lace, and then I came to a path that led up to a gate at the top of the ridge. There was a fairly fresh manure pile in the path, and I stopped to watch two tumblebugs at work. They shaped their ball, rolled it onto the path, and started down the hill with it, the one in front walking on its forelegs and tugging the ball along with its hind legs, the one in the back walking on its hind legs and pushing the ball with its forelegs. For a while I lost myself in poking around on my hands and knees, looking at the other small creatures who lived in the grass: the ants, the beetles, the worms, the butterflies who sought the manure piles or the flowers, the bees that were working in the clover. Snakes lived in the field too, and rabbits and mice and meadowlarks and sparrows and bobwhites, but I wasn't so likely to come upon those by crawling around and parting the grass with my hands.

After a while I went on up to the gate, and through it, and across the ridge to the pond. That field was the one we called the Pond Field. Grandpa said that when he took over the farm as a young man, that field had been ill used and there were many gullies in it. He had made the pond by working back and forth across a big sinkhole, first with a breaking plow, and then with a slip-scraper in which he hauled the loosened earth to the gullies and filled them. And thus he restored the field at the same time that he dug the pond. A breeze was moving over the pond, covering the surface with little shards and splinters of blue sky. I shucked off my sweaty clothes and laid them in the grass.

Fred Brightleaf and Henry and I were absolutely forbidden to swim in the pond, or anyplace else, without a grownup along. We were absolutely, absolutely forbidden to go swimming alone, without at least another boy on hand to tell where we had drowned. My poor mother, terrified by my transgressions, attempted to keep me alive until grown by a remedy known in our family as "peach tree tea"—a peach (or lilac) switch applied vigorously to the shanks of the legs. This caustic medication inflicted great suffering on me and on her, and produced not the slightest correction in my behavior. If she had been able to whip me *while* I was swimming, then the pain might have overridden the pleasure and destroyed my willfulness. But since her punishment was necessarily distant from my immersions, the pleasure outweighed the pain and lasted longer. Back there at the pond by myself I could maintain for at least a while the illusion that I was no more than myself, Andy Catlett, as ancestorless as the first creature, neither the son of Bess and Wheeler Catlett nor the grandson of Dorie and Marce Catlett and Mat and Margaret Feltner.

I crossed the rim of deep cattle tracks at the edge of the pond and waded in, feeling the muddy bottom grow soft and miry underfoot. When I was in knee-deep I launched myself flat out, smacked down, went under, came up, and swam my best overhand stroke out toward the middle. If Fred and Henry had been there we would have raced. Being alone, I took my time. When I got out to the deep place I sucked in a big breath and dived. Way down where the water was black and cold it was revealed to me that if I drowned before I lived to be grown I would be sorry, and I kicked and stroked at the dark, watching the water brighten until my head broke out into daylight and air again.

I swam back into shallow water. This partial concession to my mother's fears made me feel absolved without confession, forgiven without regret. I turned over on my back and floated for a long time. Looked at from so near the surface of the pond, the sky was huge, the world almost nothing at all, and I apparently absent altogether. The sky seemed a great gape of vision, without the complication of so much as an eye. Now and then a butterfly or a snake doctor or a bird would fly across and I would watch it. But what really fascinated and satisfied me were the birds high up that, after you had looked into the sky a while, just appeared or were just there: a hawk soaring, maybe, or a swift or a swallow darting about.

There were three joys of swimming. The first was going down out of the hot air into the cooling water. The second was being in the water. The third was coming out again. After I was cooled and quiet, a little tired, and had begun to dislike the way my fingertips had wrinkled, I waded out into the breeze that was chilly now on my wet skin. I stood in the grass and let the breeze dry me, shivering a little until I felt the warmth of the sun. And maybe the best joy of all, a fourth, was the familiar feeling of my clothes when I put them on again.

For a long time then I just sat in the grass, feeling clean and content, thinking perhaps of nothing at all. I was nine years old, going on ten; having never needed to ask, I knew exactly where I was; I did not want to be anyplace else.

2

What moved me finally was hunger. I thought of the bowl of cold biscuits that Grandma kept covered with a plate in the dish cabinet. If she was in the kitchen when I got there, she would butter me two and fill them with jam. If she was not in the kitchen, I would just take two or three from the bowl and eat them as they were, and that would be good enough.

When I came over the ridge behind the house and barns and started down toward the lot gate, I was pretending to be a show horse. Our father had taken Henry and me to the Shelby County Fair not long before. We had watched the horse show in the old round wooden arena, and I had brought home a program that I read over and over to savor the fine names of the horses. And often when I was out by myself I did the gaits.

It was not apparent to me how a two-legged creature could perform the slow gait or rack, but I could do very credible versions, I thought, of the walk, trot, and canter. And so I was a three-gaited horse, light sorrel, very fine in my conformation and motion and style. And I was the rider of the horse I was. And I was the announcer who said, "Ladies and gentlemen, please ask your horses to canter."

I saw my grandfather then. He was on Rose, his bay mare, coming around the corner of the barn toward the lot gate. He let himself through the gate and shut it again without dismounting, and started up the rise toward me. He was eighty that summer; his walking cane hung by its crook from his right forearm. He had the mare in a brisk running walk.

From where I watched, except for the cane, you would have thought him no older than my father. Afoot, he was clearly an old man; on horseback he recovered something of the force and grace of his younger days, and you could see what he had been. He rode as a man rides who has forgotten he is on a horse.

As we drew near to each other, I slowed to a walk and then changed to a trot, which I thought my best gait, wanting him to be pleased. But his countenance, set and stern as it often was, did not change. He reined the mare in only a little.

"Baby, go yonder to the house. Your daddy wants you."

"Why?" I knew he wouldn't tell me, but I asked anyhow.

"Ne' mind! He wants to talk to you."

He put his heel to the mare and went by and on up toward the ridgetop. He rode looking straight ahead. The wind carried the mare's tail out a little to the side and snatched puffs of dust from her footfalls. I watched until first the mare and then he went out of sight over the ridge.

I did not enjoy transactions that began "Your daddy wants to talk to you." I did not cherish the solemn precincts of the grown-up world in which such transactions took place. But I had no choice now, having heard, and I went on to the house. In my guilt I supposed my father had somehow learned of my trip to the pond.

There was nobody in the kitchen; it was quiet; a cloth was spread over the dishes on the table; the afternoon sunlight came into the room through the open pantry door. I went through the back hall to the front of the house. When I came into the living room I was surprised to see Cousin Thelma there, dressed up. She was Grandma's sister's child, about my father's age, forty-five or so. She and my father were sitting in rocking chairs, talking quietly. I do not know where my grandmother was.

When I opened the door my father and Cousin Thelma quit talking. Cousin Thelma smiled at me and said, "Hello, Andy, my sweet."

My father smiled at me too, but he did not say anything. He stood, held out his hand to me, and I took it. He led me out into the hall and up the stairs.

And I remember how terribly I did not want to go. I had come in out of the great free outdoor world of my childhood—the world in which, in my childish fantasies, I hoped someday to be a man. But my father, even more than my mother with her peach switch, was the messenger of another world, in which, as I unwillingly knew, I was already involved in expectation and obligation, difficulty and sorrow. It was as if I knew this even from my father's smile, from the very touch of his hand. Later I would understand how surely even then he had begun to lead me to some of the world's truest pleasures, but I was far from such understanding then.

We went back to the room over the dining room. My father shut the door soundlessly and sat down on the bed. I stood in front of him. He was still holding my hand, as though it were something he had picked up and forgotten to put down.

"Andy," he said, "Uncle Andrew was badly hurt this afternoon. A fellow shot him. I want you to understand. It may be he won't be able to live."

He was looking straight at me, and I saw something in his eyes I never had seen there before: fear — fear and grief. For what I felt then I had, and have, no name. It was something like embarrassment, as if I had blundered into knowledge that was forbidden to small boys. I knew the disturbance my father had felt in imparting it to me; this made me feel that something was required of me, and I did not know what. That Uncle Andrew was a man who could be shot had not occurred to me before, but I could not say that.

What I said sounded to me as odd and inane, probably, as anything else I might have said: "Where did he get shot?"

"Down at Stoneport."

"I mean where did he get hit?"

"Once above the belt and once below." And my father touched his own belly in the places of Uncle Andrew's wounds. Now, when I remember, it sometimes seems to me that he touched those places on my own belly — certainly, in the years to come, I would touch them myself — and perhaps he did. "Here," he said, "and here."

"Did you see him?"

"Yes. I've been to the hospital, and I saw him."

"What did he say?" I was trying, I think, to call him back, not from death, but from strangeness, the terrible distinction of his hurt, into which he was now withdrawn.

"He said a fellow shot him."

And I did then have at least the glimpse of a vision of Uncle Andrew lying on a bed, saying such words to my father who stood beside him.

What more we said and how we left that room I do not remember.

Now I know that my father led me away to keep me, in my first knowledge of what had happened, away from Grandma in her first knowledge of it—as if to reduce grief by dividing it. Also I think he was moved by a hopeless instinct to protect me, to shield me from the very thing he had to tell me, before which he was himself helpless and unprotected.

Somehow I got out of the house again. As I stepped around the corner of the back porch, Jarrat Coulter and Dick Watson drove up to the barn lot gate in Cousin Jarrat's scratched and dusty car. They had been to town to get Grandpa's broken hay rope spliced; there was hay to be put up the next day.

I ran to greet them. Both of them were my friends, and I was happy to see them. I needed something ordinary to happen.

They were looking out at me, smiling. Ordinarily Cousin Jarrat would have said, "Andy, how about opening the gate, old bud?"

But I violated my own wish for the ordinary by stepping up on the running board and announcing, "Uncle Andrew got shot."

They had already heard—I could see that they had—but in their confusion they pretended that they had not.

Dick said nothing, and Cousin Jarrat said, "Aw! Is that a fact? Well!"

And then the day seemed to collapse around me into what it had become. There was no place where what had happened had not happened.

Later, I remember, I was standing in the little pantry off the kitchen, watching my grandmother at work. In the pantry was the table covered by a broken marble dresser-top where she rolled out the dough for biscuits or pie crusts, and so she must have been making biscuits or a pie, though it is not clear to me why she should have been doing that at such a time. I suppose that, in her trouble, she had needed to put herself to work. Perhaps she thought she was distracting or comforting me. She knew at least how I loved to watch her at work there, especially when she made pies: rolling out the dough for the bottom crust and pressing it into the pan, pouring in the filling, crisscrossing the long strips of dough over the top, and then holding the pan on the fingertips of her left hand while she stroked a knife around the edge, cutting off the overhanging bits of dough.

The sun, getting low, shone in at the one window of the pantry, and everything it touched gleamed a rich reddish gold. I stood at her elbow, as I had done many times, and watched and we talked, about what I cannot imagine. My father must have been gone for some time. Cousin Thelma, if she was still there, was in the living room. My grandfather had not returned.

And then my other grandfather, Mat Feltner, rapped at the kitchen door and came in. He had come, he said, to take me home. I remember him and Grandma smiling, speaking pleasantly, looking down at me.

I followed my grandfather out to his car. We got in and started down toward Hargrave. We had gone maybe two miles when Granddaddy, who had driven so far in silence, laid his hand on my knee, as he would do sometimes, and said, "Hon, your uncle Andrew is dead. He died about five o'clock."

I did not reply, and he said no more. He was a comforting man to be with. Perhaps that was enough.

The sun was down by the time we got to Hargrave. Granddaddy pulled up in front of our house, and I got out. Where he went then, I do not know.

Henry and our friends Tim and Bubby Kentfield and Noah Burk were standing in the front yard. They gathered around me.

"Uncle Andrew got killed," Henry said.

I said I knew it. They were all looking at me, solemn-faced and excited at the same time.

"I know it," I said. "Granddaddy told me."

There we were, all of us together as we often were, and yet changed, and none of us knew what to do.

"Well. What are we going to do?" Henry said.

"The man that killed him's name's Carp Harmon," Noah Burk said. "He shot him with a .38 pistol."

"Carp Harmon," I said.

"They got him in the jail right now."

I went on into the house—looking, I suppose, for something that was the same as before. But neither of my parents was in the house. Nor were my sisters. The kitchen was full of women who had come to help or bring food. They were putting things away, sort of taking over, the way they would do.

"Hello, Andy hon," they said. They gave me hugs. They were treating me like somebody special, which made them seem strange. And their presence in the house without at least my mother there made *it* seem strange.

Miss Iris Flynn said, "Honey, I loved your uncle Andrew. We'll miss him, won't we?" She bit her underlip and looked away.

Some of the others said things too. It was a little as though they wanted to ensure that their love would last by telling it to somebody young.

I wanted to be able to think of something proper to say. It came to me that if I had been a grown man I probably could have thought of something. I would have comforted them.

"Well, good-bye," I said. "I reckon I'm going outdoors." And I went out.

"Come on," Henry said. He was the youngest one of us, but nobody held back to argue. We all went out to the street and started down into town.

I don't know where any of our grown-ups were. They were somewhere else, struck down or disappeared. The streets were empty. It was late in the evening, a weekday, and everybody was at home, eating supper maybe, or getting ready for bed, or sitting on porches or in backyards, cooling off. But to us, to me at least, it seemed that the life of the town had drawn back and hushed in wonder and sorrow that Uncle Andrew was dead. It was as if the people withdrew and hid themselves in deference to us boys who used to devil Uncle Andrew to take us swimming, which he had sometimes done. In the warm, slowly dimming twilight, nothing was abroad in the town except the pigeons clapping their wings about the courthouse tower and our little band walking bunched together to the jail. Nobody saw us. It seems to me that, for the time being, not even a car passed. The river flowed solemnly by as if strictly minding its own business.

The jail adjoined the back of the courthouse, its tall stone-barred facade set back a little behind an iron fence. When we got there we just stopped and looked at it, as though at that moment an immense reality, that we would not be done with for a long time, first laid hold on us. Uncle Andrew had been killed. Somewhere inside the jail, only a few feet from us, was the man who had killed him. For a long time there was nothing to be done but stand there in the large silence and the failing light, and know and know the thing we knew.

And then, filling his eight-year-old voice with a bravado that astonished me and perhaps astonished him, Henry called out at the front of the jail and its padlocked iron door: "Carp Harmon, you son of a bitch, come out of there!"

3

After dark that night somebody took Henry and me to Granny and Granddaddy Feltner's house up at Port William. I do not know which of the grown-ups had decided that we would be better off there, but I am sure they were right. On the way to Port William we stopped at Grandma and Grandpa Catlett's, I suppose to let me get my extra clothes and whatever else I had left.

While we were there one of the grown-ups said to me, "Don't you think you ought to go speak to your grandma?" It would have been like my father to say that, and he may have been there, but I don't remember. It could have been Aunt Lizzie, Grandma's sister. This was fifty years ago, and I have forgotten some things. But I must have been too filled with astonishment and alarm even to have noticed some things that I wish now I could remember.

I remember climbing the stairs again, by myself this time, and going into the bedroom where my grandmother was. She was in the dark, alone. I could barely see her lying motionless on the old iron bed. Her stillness touches me yet. She seemed to lie beneath the violence that had, in striking Uncle Andrew, struck her and struck us all, and now she merely submitted to it, signifying to herself by her stillness that there was nothing at all that could be done.

What had happened to us could only be suffered now, and we would be suffering it a long time; I knew that as soon as I entered the room. I had been sent perhaps with the hope that seeing me might be of some comfort to her, but I remember how swiftly I knew that she could not be comforted. Comfortlessness had come and occupied the house. She had been felled, struck down, and there she was, greatly needing comfort where there was no comfort. I walked over to the bed and stood beside it.

She must have recognized my footsteps, for she said in a voice that I would not have recognized as hers if it had not come from her, "Oh, honey, we'll never see your Uncle Andrew again. We never will see him anymore."

❧

Perhaps it was the next day that Henry and I, dressed in our Sunday clothes this time, were taken back to Hargrave, stopping again at Grandma and Grandpa Catlett's, why I do not know. It was a sunny morning. The hushed old house was occupied by the usual population of neighbors come to do what they could. I remember only my Grandfather Catlett sitting in the swing on the back porch, wearing his straw hat as he was apt to do even in the house, forgetting to take it off, his hands clasped over the crook of his cane. Cousin Thelma was sitting beside him. She was smiling, speaking to him with a wonderful attentiveness. He was trying, I remember, to respond in kind, and yet he could not free himself of his thoughts; you could tell it by his eyes.

When we got to our house at Hargrave we did not see our father and we did not see Aunt Judith, Uncle Andrew's wife. The house was full of flowers and quiet people, who got even quieter when they saw us. Our mother, smiling, met us at the door and welcomed us, almost as if we were guests, into the front room, which had been utterly changed to make way for the coffin that stood on its trestle against the wall farthest from the door.

Our mother led us over to the coffin and stood with us while we looked. Lying in the coffin, dressed up, his eyes shut and his hands still with the stillness of death, was Uncle Andrew. And so I knew for sure.

Henry and I seemed to be like people walking in what had been a forest after a terrific storm. Our grown-ups, who until then had stood protectingly over us, had fallen, or they were diminished by the simple, sudden presence of calamity. We seemed all at once to have become tall; it was not a pleasant distinction.

❧

We stayed at Port William in the care of Nettie Banion, Granny Feltner's cook, while Granny and Granddaddy and our aunt Hannah went to Hargrave for Uncle Andrew's funeral. When we heard the car returning into the driveway, we went around the house to meet them. Granny and Granddaddy greeted us as if it were just an ordinary day and we were there on an ordinary visit. It was a kind pretense that became almost a reality, something they were good at.

But Hannah, who was young and not yet skilled in grief, could not belie the actual day that it was. Tears came into her eyes when she saw us. Forcing herself to smile, she said, "Boys, he looked just like he was asleep."

Hannah was married to our Uncle Virgil, who was away in the war. She was beautiful, I thought, and I imagined that someday I might marry a woman just like her. She was always nice to Henry and me, and it was not just because she loved Uncle Virgil who loved us; she was nice to us because she loved us herself. I was far from seeing any comfort in what she said to us about Uncle Andrew; I knew he was in no ordinary sleep. But it was good of her to say it, and I knew that as well.

When all this happened I was younger almost than I can imagine now. It is hard for me to recall exactly what I felt. I think that I did not grieve in the knowing and somewhat theoretical way of grown people, who say to themselves, for example, that a death of some sort awaits us all, and who may have understood in part how the order of time is shaped and held within the order of eternity. I had no way of generalizing or conceptualizing my feelings. It seems to me now that I had no sympathy for myself.

Only once do I remember attempting in any outward or verbal way to own my loss. I admired a girl named Marian Davis who was in my room at school. One afternoon in the fall of the year of Uncle Andrew's death, we were walking home in the crowd of boys and girls that straggled out along the street. Marian was walking slightly in front of me. All at once it came to me that I might enlarge myself in her eyes by attaching to myself the tragedy that had befallen my family. I stepped up beside her and said, "Marian, I reckon you heard about Uncle Andrew." Perhaps she had not heard—that did not occur to me. I thought that she had heard but was dumbfounded by my clumsy attempt to squander my feelings; perhaps she even sensed that I was falsifying them in order to squander them. She pretended not to hear. She did not look at me. In her silence a fierce shame came upon me that did not wear away for years. I did not try again to speak of Uncle Andrew's death to anyone until I was grown.

Perhaps I did not grieve in the usual sense at all. The world that I knew had changed into a world that I knew only in part; perhaps I understood that I would not be able ever again to think of it as a known world. My awareness of my loss must have been beyond summary. It must have been exactly commensurate with what I had lost, and what I had lost was Uncle Andrew as I had known him, my life with Uncle Andrew. I had lost what I remembered.

4

I was Uncle Andrew's namesake, and I had come to be his buddy. "My boy," he would call me when he was under the influence not only of the considerable tenderness that was in him but of what I now know to have been bourbon whiskey.

When I first remember him, Uncle Andrew and Aunt Judith were living in Columbia, South Carolina, where Uncle Andrew was a traveling salesman for a hardware company. They came home usually once in the summer and again at Christmas. They would come by train, and my father would take Henry and me and go to meet them. When Aunt Judith came early and Uncle Andrew made the trip alone, he would not always arrive on the train we met. I remember standing with Henry on the station platform while our father hurriedly searched through the train on which Uncle Andrew was supposed to have arrived. I remember our disappointment, and our father's too brief explanation that Uncle Andrew must have missed the train, leaving us to suppose that when he missed it Uncle Andrew had been breathlessly trying to catch it. In fact, he may have missed it by a very comfortable margin; he may have been in circumstances in which he did not remember that he had a train to catch.

His and Aunt Judith's arrival, anyhow, certainly made life more interesting for Henry and me. Aunt Judith, who was childless, was affectionate and indulgent—in need of our affection, as she was of everybody's, and willing to spoil us for it. Uncle Andrew was so unlike anybody else we knew as to seem a species of one. He was capable of adapting his speech and manners to present company if he wanted to, but he did not often want to. He talked to us boys as he talked to everybody else, and in that way he charmed us. To us, he seemed to exist always at the center of his own uproar, carrying on in a way that was restless, reckless, humorous, and loud. One Christmas—it must have been 1939—Henry and I conceived the idea of giving him a cigarette tin filled with rusty nails. Our mother wrapped it prettily for us and put his name on it. A perfect actor, he received it with a large display first of gratitude and affection, and then, as he opened it, of curiosity, anticipation, surprise, indignation, and outrage. He administered a burlesque spanking and stomping to each of our "bee-hinds," as he called them, uttering throughout the performance a commentary of grunts, raspberries, and various profane exclamations. Thus he granted success to our trick.

At about that time his drinking seems to have become a problem again. My father, who could not rest in the presence of a problem—who in fact was possessed by visions of solutions—decided that Uncle Andrew should come home and farm. Borrowing the money, my father bought two farms, one that we continued to call the Mack Crayton Place about five miles from Hargrave, and another, the Will Bower Place, adjoining Grandma and Grandpa Catlett's place nearer to Port William. Uncle Andrew, according to the plan they made, would look after the farms while my father concentrated on his law practice. My father sent Uncle Andrew enough money to buy a 1940 Chevrolet, and Uncle Andrew and Aunt Judith came home. Uncle Andrew was then forty-five years old, five years older than my father.

That homecoming gave me a new calling and a new career. Uncle Andrew and Aunt Judith rented a small apartment in a house belonging to an old doctor in Hargrave. Uncle Andrew began his daily trips to the farms, and I began wanting to go with him. I was six years old, and going with him became virtually the ruling purpose of my life. When I was not in school or under some parental bondage, I was likely to be with him. On the days I went with him, the phone would ring at our house before anybody was up. I would run down the stairs, put the receiver to my ear, and Uncle Andrew's voice would say, "Come around, baby."

I would hang up without replying, get into my clothes as fast as I could, and hurry through the backstreets to the apartment, where Aunt Judith would have breakfast ready. She made wonderful plum jelly and she knew I liked it; often she would have it on the table for me. Uncle Andrew called coffee "java," and when Aunt Judith asked him how he wanted his eggs, he would say, "Two lookin' atcha!" singing it out, as he did all his jazzy slang.

To me, there was something exotic about the two of them and their apartment. I had never known anybody before who lived in an apartment; the idea had a flavor of urbanity that was new and strange to me. Uncle Andrew and Aunt Judith had lived in distant places, in cities, that they sometimes talked about. They had been to the South Carolina seashore, and Uncle Andrew had fished in Charleston Harbor. I had never seen the ocean and I loved to quiz them about it. Could you actually ride the waves? How did you do it? If you looked straight out over the ocean, how far could you see? I could not get enough of the thought that you could not see across it. Besides all that, Aunt Judith was the only woman I knew who smoked cigarettes, and this complicated the smell of her perfume in a way I rather liked.

We would eat breakfast and talk while the early morning brightened outside the kitchen window, and they would smoke, and Uncle Andrew would say, "Gimme one mo' cup of that java, Miss Judy-pooty."

Finally we would leave, and then began what always seemed to me the day's adventure; I knew more or less what to expect at breakfast, but when you were loose in the world with Uncle Andrew you did not know what to expect.

The Chevrolet was inclined to balk at the start, and Uncle Andrew would stomp the accelerator and stab the engine furiously with the choke. "That's right! Cough," he would say, stomping and stabbing, "you one-lunged son of a bitch!" And the car would buck out of the driveway and up the low rise like a young horse. He treated all machines as if they were recalcitrant and uncommonly stupid draft animals. When the car, under his abuse, finally learned its lesson and began to run smoothly, he would look over at me, screwing his face up and talking through his nose —in the style, probably, of some cabdriver he remembered: "Where to, college?"

"Oh," I would say, laughing, "up to the Crayton Place, I reckon."

Of the two farms, Uncle Andrew much preferred the Crayton Place, where Jake and Minnie Branch lived — and so, of course, I preferred it too. The Bower Place was perhaps a little too close to Grandpa Catlett's; also the tenant there, Jake Branch's brother, was a quiet, rather solitary man who thought mostly of keeping his two boys at work and of staying at work himself. But at the Crayton Place, what with Jake's children and Minnie's children and Jake's and Minnie's children and whichever two or three of Minnie's six brothers Jake had managed to lure in (or bail out of jail) as hired hands, together with the constant passing in and out of more distant relations, neighbors, and friends, there was always commotion, always the opportunity for talk and laughter and carrying on. Some rowdy joke or tale could get started there and go on for two or three days, retold and elaborated for every newcomer, restlessly egged on — over the noisy objections and denials of whoever was the butt of it — by pretended casual comments or questions asked in mock innocence. Minnie never knew the number she would feed at a meal. I have seen her put biscuits on the table in a wash pan, three dozen at a time.

✳

Perhaps Uncle Andrew had some affection for farming. He had, after all, been raised to it — or Grandpa, anyhow, had tried to raise him to it. But he was unlike his father and my father, for whom farming was a devotion and a longing; it was not a necessity of life to him. He saw to things, purchased harness and machine parts, did whatever was needed to keep men and teams and implements in working order, and helped out where help was needed. But what he really loved was company, talk, some kind of to-do, something to laugh at.

When our association began, I appointed myself his hired hand at a wage of a quarter a day. Since I was not big enough to do most of the jobs I wanted to do, I tended to spend the days in an uneasy search for something I could do to justify my pay. I served him mostly as a sort of page, running errands, carrying water, opening gates, handing him things. Occasionally he or Jake Branch would dignify me with a real job, sending me to the tobacco patch with a hoe or letting me drive a team on the hayrake. But Uncle Andrew never let my wages become a settled issue. Sometimes he paid me willingly enough. Sometimes I would have to argue, beg, and bully to get him even to acknowledge that he had ever heard of the idea of paying me. When the subject came up in front of a third party, he would say, "It's worth a quarter a day just to have him with me." That confused me, for I treasured the compliment and yet felt that it devalued my "work."

One day when he and I were helping Jake Branch set tobacco on a stumpy hillside, a terrific downpour came upon us. R. T. and Ester Purlin, two of Minnie's children from her first marriage, and I were dropping the plants into previously marked rows, and the men were coming behind us, rapidly setting them in the rain-wet ground, all of us working barefoot to save our shoes. When the new hard shower suddenly began, we all ran to the shelter of the trees that grew along the hollow at the foot of the slope. Uncle Andrew and I stood beneath a sort of arbor made by a wild grapevine whose leaves had grown densely over the top of a small tree. For a while it was an almost perfect umbrella. And then, as the rain fell harder, the foliage began to leak. The day was chilly as well as wet, and Uncle Andrew was wearing a canvas hunting coat, which he now opened and spread like a hen's wing. "Here, baby," he said. I ducked under and he closed me in. For a long time I stood there, dark and dry in his warmth, in his mingled smell of sweat and pipe tobacco, while the rain fell hard around us and splattered on the ground at our feet.

In the winter when nightfall came early, he would often stop by our house as he was going home. He would come in and sit down. My father would lay aside the evening paper, and they would talk quietly and companionably, going over the stages of work on the farms, saying what had been done and what needed doing. Uncle Andrew would have on his winter clothes: an old felt hat, corduroys, the tan canvas hunting coat, and under that a lined suede jacket with a zipper. He would not take off his outdoor clothes because he was on his way to supper and did not intend to stay long. I would climb into his lap and make myself comfortable. Perhaps I appeared to be listening, but what I was really doing was smelling. There was the smell of Uncle Andrew himself, which was a constant and always both comforting and exciting, but on those evenings his clothes gave off also the cold smells of barns and animals, hay and

tobacco, ground grain, wood smoke. Those smells charmed me utterly
and saddened me, for they told me what I had missed by being in school.

"Take me with you in the morning," I would say.

And he would say, "Can't do it, college." Or, in another mood, he
would give me a hug and a pat. "I wish I could, baby, but you got to go to
school."

For children his term of endearment, which also was Grandpa's, was
"baby." He called me that when he felt tender toward me, as he often did,
nearly always when he was drinking but often too when he was not.

He might have wanted a boy of his own, I sometimes thought, and
maybe I was the kind of boy he wanted. At school I took to signing myself
"Andrew Catlett, Jr." Sometimes it seemed unfair to me that I was not
his son. I wanted to be a man just like him.

I liked his rough way of joking and carrying on. Often when I showed
up at his apartment, he would say in his nasal slang, "Hello, bozo! Gimme
five!" And we would do a big handshake.

His term of emphatic agreement was "Yowza!" Or he would say, "Aw
yeah!"—pronounced as one word: "Aw'eah!"—which was both affirma-
tive and derisive. He could make one word perform lots of functions.

Anybody dead and buried, especially any of Aunt Judith's relatives,
was "planted in the skull orchard."

Anybody licked or done in had been "nailed to the cross."

His threats to Henry and me, even when somewhat meant, were
delivered with a burlesque of ferocity that made us laugh: "I'm going to
stomp your bee-hind!" he would say. "I'm going to rap on your ding-
dong! I'm going to cloud up and rain all over you! I'm going to get you
down and work on you!"

He would sometimes put on Henry's or my straw hat, much too small
for him, insert an old magnifying lens in his eye as a monocle, look at us,
and say, "Redwood fer dittos, college!" What that meant I do not know; I
don't know even if those are the right words. That was what it sounded
like. Wearing the "monocle" and tiny-looking hat, speaking sentences
imitated, I suppose, from somebody he had run across somewhere away,
he could transform himself, sometimes a little scarily, into somebody we
had never seen before. Leering and mouthing, carrying on an outrageous

blather of profanity and nonsense, he could make us laugh until we were lying on the floor, purged, exhausted, aching, and still laughing.

We had a mongrel bull terrier bitch named Nosey that he did not especially care for. Somebody told us we ought to bob her tail. As we did with all out-of-the-way propositions, we laid this one before Uncle Andrew.

"Uncle Andrew, do you know how to cut off Nosey's tail?"

"Why, hell *yes!*" he said, opening his pocketknife, "I'll cut it off right behind her ears."

And then he mimed the whole procedure, whooping and making raspberries, laughing at himself, until it was funny even to us.

☘

Sometimes, for reasons unclear to us then, he would feel bad and need to sleep. In Jake Branch's yard under the big white oak, or in the woods at the Bower Place, or on the shady side of one or another of the barns, he would open both doors of the car, stretch out on the front seat, and sleep an hour or two, or all afternoon. I would be utterly mystified and even offended. How could anybody sleep when there were so many things to do?

Or Henry and I would bring Bubby Kentfield and Noah Burk and maybe two or three more around to the apartment on a Sunday afternoon and find him asleep on the couch.

We would tramp into the room in a body, like a delegation, assuming that if he was not in a good mood, we could get him into one. We believed that there was strength in numbers.

"Uncle Andrew, we was wondering if you'd take us swimming."

"Yeah, Uncle Andrew, we want to go to the quarry."

He would turn his head reluctantly and look at us. "Aw God, boys, you all don't need to go swimming."

"Yes, we do. It's hot."

"Well, go on then!"

"Well, we need you to go with us."

"No, you don't."

"Yes, we do. Mother said if you went, we could go."

"Suppose you drown."

"She thinks you won't let us drown."

"The hell I won't!"

"Well, are you coming?"

"Go on, now, damn it! Get out of here! Go do something else."

He would fold his hands and shut his eyes, the picture of hope defeated.

Sometimes he would be quiet and sad-seeming. Always at those times he sang the same song:

> *Missed the Saturday dance*
> *Heard they crowded the floor*
> *Couldn't bear it without you*
> *Don't get around much anymore.*

Was there, somewhere, a woman he missed, or was he mindful that he was getting older, or did he just like the song? He had a good voice, and he sang well.

✾

For fifty years and more I have been asking myself, What was he? What manner of a man? For I have never been sure. There are things that I remember, things that I have heard, and things that I am able (a little) to imagine. But what he was seems always to be disappearing a step or two beyond my thoughts.

He was, for one thing, a man of extraordinary good looks. He had style, not as people of fashion have it (though he had the style of fashion when he wanted it), but as, for example, certain horses have it: a self-awareness so complete as to be almost perfectly unconscious, realized in acts rather than thoughts. He wore his clothes with that kind of style. He looked as good in work clothes, I thought, as he did dressed up. Clothes did not matter much to me, and yet I remember being proud to be with him when he was dressed up—in a light summer suit, say, and a straw boater—for I thought he looked better than anybody. He was a big man, six feet two inches tall and weighing a hundred and eighty pounds. He had a handsome, large-featured face with a certain fineness or sensitivity that suggested possibilities in him that he mainly ignored. His eyes, as Grandma loved to say, were "hazel," and they were very expressive, as responsive to thought as to sight. He loved ribaldry, raillery, impudence. He spoke at times a kind of poetry of vulgarity.

And yet there was something dark or troubled in him also, as though he foresaw his fate; I felt it even then. I have a memory of him with a certain set to his mouth and distance in his eyes, an expression of difficult acceptance, as if he were resigned to being himself, as if perhaps he saw what it would lead to. His silences, though never long, were sometimes solemn and preoccupied. When he was still in his twenties, his hair had begun to turn gray.

For another thing, he was as wild, probably, as any human I have ever known. He was a man, I think, who was responsive mainly to impulses: desire, affection, amusement, self-abandon, sometimes anger.

When he felt good, he would be laughing, joking, mocking, mimicking, singing, mouthing a whole repertory of subverbal noises. He would say — and as Yeager Stump later told me, he would do — anything he thought of. He would lounge, grinning, in his easy chair and talk outrageously, as if merely curious to hear what he might say.

I was in the third grade when the teachers at our school asked the students to ask their fathers to volunteer to build some seesaws on the playground. Henry and I, knowing our father would not spare the time, brought the matter before Uncle Andrew.

"Well, college," he said, "I'll take it under consideration. Tell all the women teachers to line up out by the road, and I'll drive by and look 'em over. It might be I could give 'em a little lift."

He had, I am sure, no intention of helping with the seesaws; he never had been interested in a school. But Henry, who was in the second grade, dutifully relayed the message to his teacher. I remember well the difficulty of hearing Henry's teacher repeat to my teacher Uncle Andrew's instructions. As I perfectly understood, our teachers' outrage was not necessarily contingent upon Henry's indiscretion; Uncle Andrew would have delivered his suggestion in person if the circumstances had been different and it had occurred to him to do so.

At times he seemed to be all energy, intolerant of restraint, unpredictable. His presence, for so small a boy as I was, was like that of some large male animal who might behave as expected one moment and the next do something completely unforeseen and astonishing.

One morning we went to the Bower Place only to find Charlie Branch stalled for want of a mowing machine part. We started back to Hargrave to get the part, Uncle Andrew driving complacently along at the wartime speed limit, and I chinning the dashboard as usual. We got to a place where the road went down through a shallow cut with steep banks on both sides, and all of a sudden Chumpy and Grover Corvin stepped into the road in front of us. Chumpy and Grover were just big teenage boys then, but they were already known as outlaws and bullies; a lot of people were afraid of them. They wanted a ride, and by stepping into the road they meant to force Uncle Andrew to stop. What he did was clap the accelerator to the floor and drive straight at them. His response was as instantaneous and all-out as that of a kicking horse. He ran them out of the road and up the bank, cutting away at the last split second. We drove on as before. He did not say a word.

5

While Uncle Andrew farmed and did whatever else he did, Aunt Judith and her mother busied themselves with the care and maintenance of the Hargrave upper crust. Aunt Judith's mother had been born a Hargrave, a descendant of the Hargrave for whom the town was named, and so Aunt Judith was virtually a Hargrave herself. By blood she was only a quarter Hargrave, but by disposition and indoctrination she was 100 percent, as her mother expected and perhaps required. The two of them belonged to the tightly drawn little circle (almost a knot) of the female scions of the first families of Hargrave — a complex cousinship that preserved and commended itself in an endless succession of afternoon bridge parties. At these functions everybody was "cud'n" somebody: Cud'n Anne, Cud'n Nancy, Cud'n Charlotte, Cud'n Phoebe, and so on. Theirs was an exclusive small enclosure that one could not enter or leave except by birth and death. My mother, for example, was excluded for the original sin of having been born in Port William — an exclusion which I believe she understood as an escape.

This feminine inner circle had of course a masculine outer circle to which Uncle Andrew pertained by marriage and in which he participated (being incapable of silence, let alone deference) by snorts, hoots, spoofs, jokes, and other blasphemies. He was particularly intrigued by the fervent cousinship of the little class that he had wedded, and he loved to enlarge it by addressing as "cud'n" or "cuz" any bootblack, barfly, yardman, panhandler, dishwasher, porter, or janitor he happened to encounter in the presence of his wife and mother-in-law. His favorite name for Aunt Judith was "Miss Judy-pooty," but he also called her "Cud'n Pud'n." Her mother he named "Miz Gotrocks" in mockery of her love of elaborate costume jewelry and big hats, and her little pair of pinch-nose glasses on a silver chain. But he also called her, as occasion required, "Cud'n Mothah" and "Momma-pie." The latter name, because we children picked it up from him, was what everybody in our family came to call her.

Aunt Judith, as I judge from a set of photographs that used to hang in Momma-pie's bedroom, had been a pretty girl. She was an only child, raised by her divorced mother, who had been an only daughter. Aunt Judith and Momma-pie were a better matched pair than Aunt Judith and Uncle Andrew. Aunt Judith had grown up in the protective enclosure prescribed by Momma-pie's status and character; Uncle Andrew had grown up in no enclosure that he could get out of. That the two of them married young and in error is plain fact. Why they got married — or, rather, why Uncle Andrew married Aunt Judith — is a question my father puzzled over in considerable exasperation for the rest of his life. He always reverted to the same theory: that Momma-pie had insidiously contrived it. A mantrap had been cunningly set and baited with the perhaps tempting virginity of Aunt Judith — and Uncle Andrew, his mind diverted to other territory, had obliged by inserting his foot. Maybe so.

Maybe so. If the theory was ever provable — and my father had no proof — the chance is long gone by now. But a story that Mary Penn told me, after I had grown up, suggests at least that Uncle Andrew was not an ecstatic bridegroom. One of Mary's cousins, a schoolmate of Uncle Andrew's, told her that on the night before his wedding Uncle Andrew got drunk and fell into a road ditch. His friends gathered around, trying to help him up.

"Aw, boys," he said, "just leave me be. When I think of what I've got to lay with tomorrow night, I'd just as soon lay here in this ditch."

He had seen his fate, and named it, and yet accepted it. Why?

However their marriage began, whatever its explanation, their unlikenesses were profound. The second mystery of their union was set forth as follows by my mother: "Did your Aunt Judith have so many health problems because your Uncle Andrew drank and ran around with other women, or did your Uncle Andrew drink and run around with other women because your Aunt Judith had so many health problems?" The answer to that question too, assuming that anybody ever knew it, has been long in the grave.

The question, anyhow, states their condition accurately enough. Aunt Judith did have a lot of health problems, some of which were very painful. Since no doctor ever found a cause or a remedy for most of them, it seems that the cause must have been in her mind, which is to say in her marriage. And perhaps also in her relationship to Momma-pie. My mother remembers that Aunt Judith never said anything without looking at Momma-pie to see if it was all right. But if Aunt Judith lived in some fear of Momma-pie, I am sure that she lived also in surprise, bewilderment, and dismay at Uncle Andrew, whom she nevertheless adored.

Sometimes Uncle Andrew could be sympathetic and tender with Aunt Judith, sorry for her sufferings, worried about her, anxious to help her solve her problems. Sometimes, unable to meet her demands for attention or sympathy with the required response, he met them instead with derision. Sometimes, I imagine, he was contrite about his offenses against her and wished to do better. But as they both surely had learned beyond unlearning or pretense, the time would invariably come when, under the spell of an impulse, he would fling her away. He would fling her away as a flying swallow flings away its shadow.

Aunt Judith always asked you for affection before you could give it. For that reason she always needed more affection than she got. She would drain the world of affection, and then, fearing that it had been given only because she had asked for it, she would have to ask for more.

"Sugah," she would say to whichever of us children had come in sight, "come here and kiss yo' Aunt Judith!" And she was capable of issuing this invitation with the broad hint that, because of her frail health, the grave might claim her before we would have a chance to kiss her again. I am glad to remember that, in spite of everything, I felt a genuine affection for her, especially in the time before Uncle Andrew's death—before fate authenticated her predisposition to woe. In those days she could be a pleasant companion for a small boy, and I remember afternoons when we sat together while she read to me from the evening paper a reporter's serialized account of the movement of a group of soldiers from training camp to troopship to battle. We both became deeply interested in those articles and looked forward to them. I remember how our reading fitted together

our interest in the story of the soldiers, our sense of great history unfold-
ing, and our mutual affection and pleasure. And yet when she turned
toward me with her need, as sooner or later she always did, it was hard to
provide a response satisfactory to either of us. It is hard to give the final
kiss of this earthly life over and over again. Mostly I submitted silently to
her hugs, kisses, and other attentions, profiting the best I could from that
exotic smell of cigarette smoke and perfume that hung about her.

Her tone of self-reference almost always carried an overtone of self-
pity. She asked for pity as she asked for affection — and her demand, as
was inevitable in that hopeless emotional economy of hers, always out-
ran the available supply. As she strove forward with her various claims on
other people, she more and more destroyed the possibility of a genuine
mutuality with anybody. Her need for love isolated and estranged her
from everybody who might have loved her, and from everybody who did.

In her self-centeredness and her constant appeal to others to fulfill
her unfulfillable needs, she was like Momma-pie. Both of them, I think,
belonged to a lineage of spoiled women. From the time of her divorce,
Momma-pie had lived with her expansive pretensions in a small room at
the Broadfield Hotel on the income from a moderately good farm that
she had never seen except from the road. During her life at the hotel she
did nothing for herself except for the light and polite housekeeping of
her room. Aunt Judith was a fastidious housekeeper and a good cook—
she and Uncle Andrew had never had the money for household help—
but her work always bore the implication of her poor health, and hints
were often passed between her and Momma-pie that whatever she did
she was not quite able to do.

The would-be aristocracy of the Hargrave upper crust was, after all, I
think, a cruel burden for Aunt Judith and Momma-pie. According to the
terms that they accepted and lived by, they were important because they
were who they were. That was their axiom. And so there they were, sus-
pended in the ethereal element of their pretension, utterly estranged
from the farms and the work from which they lived, hard put to demon-
strate their usefulness to much of anybody, and forced to bear the
repeated proofs that Uncle Andrew assumed almost nothing that they
assumed.

It is pleasant and useless to wonder what might have become of Aunt

Judith if she had married a milder, more tractable man, just as it is pleasant and useless to wonder what might have become of Uncle Andrew if he had married a more robust and self-sustaining woman. Such might-have-beens only renew the notice that Aunt Judith and Uncle Andrew married each other, and in doing so joined snow and fire.

Uncle Andrew, except that he possessed "aristocratic good looks," could not have been anyone that Aunt Judith ever saw in her girlhood dreams. She must have seen him simply as she wanted to see him: a young man handsome as a prince, who would make her the envy of other girls. She must have imagined herself and him as "a beautiful couple." To Momma-pie — assuming that my father's theory of artful entrapment was correct — he must have seemed "an excellent prospect," good raw material in need of polish. If in fact they captured him, then they captured a bull in a henhouse. He was, as undoubtedly he already knew or soon found out, the very reality that their not-altogether-pretended feminine delicacy was least disposed to recognize. And now they were obliged to try to contain him in an enclosure prepared for another kind of creature. He was, whatever else he was, a man of his own time and place. He honored to some extent the conventions of his capture; he was capable of affection, sympathy, and regret. Though his confinement did not exist except when he submitted to it, sometimes he submitted to it. But he could not be held. It was not so much that he resisted or defied or rebelled against his bondage; he simply overflowed it. When he filled to his own fullness, he overflowed his confines as a rising river overflows its banks, making nothing of the boundaries and barriers that stand in its way.

The three of them made their daily lives, formed and followed their routines, made things ordinary and bearable for themselves. Their strange convergence was not a perpetual crisis. But it was nonetheless hopeless. They were two almost forceless women entangled past untangling with an almost ungentled man. He of course was as spoiled in his way as they were in theirs. They had been spoiled by generations of men who had indulged and promoted their helplessness; he had been spoiled by women who had allowed him to charm them into acceptance of his inborn unstoppability. Aunt Judith and Momma-pie had spoiled him themselves, as I think all the women in his life had done. They were under his spell, as much caught by him as he by them. They could not contain him, but they could not expel him either.

The best friend he had, I am certain, was my father, who loved him completely. But my father, purposeful and tireless, sober and passionate, in love with his family and his work, true to his obligations, could not have been Uncle Andrew's crony. They could be friends within the terms of brotherhood and partnership, but partly perhaps because he was Uncle Andrew's brother, my father was not wild; the whole budget of Catlett wildness in that generation had been allotted to Uncle Andrew. For cronies, Uncle Andrew had Buster Simms and Yeager Stump.

In his look and laugh and way of talking, Buster Simms gleefully acknowledged the world's lewdness. He was a freckled, smallish, quick-eyed man whose conversation tended to be all in tones of joking, from aggressive to kind. He called Uncle Andrew "Duke." Yeager Stump was a tall, good-looking man of somewhat the same style as Uncle Andrew. Of the three, he was the quietest. You could see in the wrinkly corners of his eyes that he was always waiting to be amused, and was being amused while he waited. Of the three, he was the only one who lived to be old.

All three felt themselves too straitly confined in marriage, and they escaped into each other's company. Or rather, each other's company was their freedom that, spent or hung over, they allowed themselves to be recaptured out of, as Samson allowed himself to be bound with seven green withes that were never dried.

"We did everything we thought of," Yeager Stump would say later. "Our only limit was our imagination."

They called each other "Cud'n Andrew" and "Cud'n Bustah" and "Cud'n Yeagah"—for ordinary use abbreviated to "Cuz"—in endless parody of the female cousinship of Hargrave.

When they met in their daily comings and goings, they would greet one another with a broad show of camaraderie and affection:

"Hello, Cuz!"

"Hello, Cuz!"

And then they would laugh. Sometimes they started laughing before they had said anything.

6

The first apartment that Uncle Andrew and Aunt Judith lived in after
they moved to Hargrave had no bathtub. Uncle Andrew loved a bathtub,
and so he would sometimes come around to our house after supper to
have a soak. That was one of the times when he and I would visit. I
would perch on the lid of the thunder jug, as he liked to call it, and he
would lie in hot water up to his chin, and we would talk. Or I would just
sit and watch him, for in everything he did he fascinated me. Unlike my
father, who was in all things thrifty and careful and neat and who bathed
vigorously like a man grooming a horse, Uncle Andrew filled the tub full
and bathed expansively, as if the tub were an ocean and he a whale. He
would bask at length in the hot water, and then he would soap and rinse
with a great heaving and sloshing and blowing and making of suds.

On one such evening, when I must have been about six or seven, I confided to him that I had fallen in love with the older sister of one of my
friends. I said that I wanted to get her off by herself somewhere — a lonely
back road, say — where we could be unobserved. I was going to say that
I would then declare my love. I had given a lot of thought and effort to
the planning of this event, but I lacked confidence; I wanted the counsel
of experience. But I got no further than that detail about the lonely back
road. For a while it looked as though Uncle Andrew might drown in the
extremity of his glee.

"Aw'eah! *Aw'eah!*" he said as he laughed and whooped and splashed.

"*Now* you're getting right, college! *Now* you're cooking with gas! You got your mind properly on your *business*! You going out *among* 'em!"

It astonishes me a little yet to realize how characteristically he did not qualify himself. I had spoken as a small boy, and he had responded unreservedly as a man, as himself. I must have loved him almost absolutely to have so confided in him. And was I hurt or disappointed when he received my confidence with such rowdy approval, infusing my shy daydream with a glandular intensity from another vision entirely? Not in the least, as far as I remember. I was bewildered, certainly, but was happy as always to have pleased him and to be carried away on the big stream of his laughter. And now, of course, I am delighted.

Later, he would quote me to his cronies. Buster Simms would lean to glance in at me where I sat beside Uncle Andrew in the car. "Duke, is he looking at the girls yet? Is he transacting any private business?"

And Uncle Andrew would declare solemnly, without looking at me, "Why, he's *got* a girl! And he tells me that his business with her calls for the strictest privacy." And he would go on. Wishing he would stop, I yet listened in fascination, understanding vaguely that they spoke of a destination at which I had not arrived but to which my fare was already paid.

Thus, though I was as innocent as Adam alone, I became aware of the sexual aura that surrounded Uncle Andrew.

He was never apart from it. He was always playing to whatever woman was at hand, whether it was Minnie Branch, wearing a pair of Jake's cast-off work shoes and with her brood in tow, or Miss Iris Flynn, who was in fact Yeager Stump's girlfriend, or Aunt Roxanna, Grandma's tall and lean oldest sister—anybody, so long as she was a woman. Or rather, he did not play to them; he lived to them, acknowledging them, requiring them to acknowledge him, as inhabitants of the same exuberantly physical and sexual world. How they responded he did not care, so long as they responded, which they invariably did. They scolded, scoffed, huffed, smiled; they reached out to him; they looked straight into his eyes and laughed. Of particular interest to me then, and still, was Uncle Andrew's friendship with Minnie Branch, for of all the people in that overflowing household on the Crayton Place, I think he liked Minnie best. For him, maybe, the female world turned on an axis held at one pole by Aunt Judith and at the other by Minnie Branch—Aunt Judith, with her bred-in dependency, her sometimes helplessness, ill with fright and self-regard, childless and forever needy; and Minnie, who was fearless, capable, hardy, fecund, unabashed, without apology or appeal. Minnie could cook and keep house for what amounted to a small hotel, split firewood, butcher a hog, raise a garden, work in the field, shoot a fox, set a hen or wring her neck. She was a large, muscular, humorous, plain-faced woman who wore a pair of steel-rimmed glasses. You could hear her laugh halfway to the back of the farm. I can see her yet with her white hens clustered at her feet, picking up shelled corn; she is leaning back against the weight of the child in her womb, fists on hips, talking and laughing.

She conceived and birthed as faithfully as a good brood cow, welcomed each newcomer without fuss, prepared without complaint for the next. There was a running joke on this subject that Uncle Andrew carried on with Minnie and Jake.

"Well, by God, Jake's been at it again! He's as hot as a boy dog!"

Minnie would throw back her head and laugh: "Haw! Haw!"

And Jake would grin and shake his head in wonder at himself. "They going to have to *do* something about me."

And when Minnie lay down on the bed, in the big, starkly furnished bedroom next to the kitchen, to suffer yet another birth, who would be there, anxiously hovering about, dispensing clean towels and hot water, eagerly bathing the infant who pretty soon appeared, but Aunt Judith and Momma-pie? They had no more to do with Minnie Branch in the ordinary course of their lives than they had to do with the farm. But Minnie's birth pangs drew them like some undeniable music, and their conversation afterward was full of the news of their participation.

Beyond the obvious reasons, Uncle Andrew liked Minnie, I think, because she made nothing special of him; she did not see him as anything unexpected. She liked him wholly and asked for nothing. He was comfortable with her.

One overcast afternoon, I remember, Uncle Andrew and I were sitting in Minnie Branch's kitchen, talking with Minnie and another woman I knew only as Mrs. Partlet. The older children and the hands, one of whom at that time was Jockey Partlet, Mrs. Partlet's husband, had been fed their dinner long ago and had gone back to the field. The firebox of the cooking range was almost cold. Uncle Andrew and I were there

perhaps just because Uncle Andrew enjoyed being there and did not particularly need to be anyplace else.

Minnie sat in a big rocking chair between the stove and the door
into the next room. She was rocking slowly back and forth, with Coreen,
her then-youngest, lying asleep in the crook of her arm. The second
youngest, Beureen, was asleep in a crib just beyond the door. Angeleen,
the third youngest, was standing quietly at Minnie's knee, looking as
though she would like to climb into her lap. At the moment, Minnie was
ignoring other people's wants. She had a chew of tobacco tucked into her
cheek and was taking her usual big part in the conversation. Now and
then she would turn her head and spit several feet into the ash bucket
behind the stove. Mrs. Partlet, a plump, pretty woman, sat in a straight
chair by the window. Her hands lay in her lap, and as the talk went on
she fiddled with her fingers. I sat at the end of the table nearest the stove
in one of the dozen or so straight chairs, no two of which were the same.
Uncle Andrew sat at the other end, by the back door, his chair tilted onto
its hind legs, his left arm lying along the edge of the table, his right hand
in his pocket. Between the stove and the window where Mrs. Partlet was
sitting, a large washtub full of soaking diapers sat on the floor.

The conversation went on casually enough for a while, and then it became humorous, and finally hilarious, carrying a sexual allusiveness that
was grown-up and powerful; even I could recognize it. They paid no more
attention to me than if I had been yet another infant too young to talk.

The laughter itself seemed to draw Uncle Andrew and Mrs. Partlet to
their feet. He extended his left hand; she granted her right. He placed his
right hand on her back and waltzed her around the room to a tune that
they both appeared to have in mind, the two of them laughing and Minnie laughing from her chair. Uncle Andrew danced Mrs. Partlet backward to the tub of soaking diapers, where to keep from falling in she had
to push against him, and she did. And then she whooped and ducked
away, still laughing, under his arm.

He looked at me. "Come on," he said. "Let's go."

The women still laughing behind us, we went out the back door and
past the well pump and the cellar wall.

And then Mrs. Partlet followed us out. "Andrew," she said.

When I looked back, Mrs. Partlet was standing in front of Uncle

Andrew, all flushed and flustered, her hands on his forearms, saying something to him that I was not supposed to hear.

He turned away, attempting to return to the hilarity of the moments before, but failing, and knowing it. "I got all the women I can take care of already."

His face as he came away was solemn-looking, as it was sometimes when he was quiet.

To him, I think, the idea of consequence was always an afterthought. He did not expect consequences; he discovered them. When he could, he laughed them away. When they pressed in through his laughter, he shut his mouth and bore them. What he had done was his fate, and so he bore it.

The second apartment that Uncle Andrew and Aunt Judith rented after they moved to Hargrave was the upstairs — three rather low-ceilinged rooms and a kitchen — of a small frame house not far from their first apartment. The new one had a bathtub. It also had two bedrooms, and so Momma-pie left her room in the Broadfield Hotel and moved in with her daughter and son-in-law. After that Uncle Andrew had to laugh more than ever to keep the consequences at bay. His home life now required him to deal constantly with two women whose dignity and self-esteem depended upon illnesses that were frequent, dramatic, and potentially fatal and that Uncle Andrew was therefore obliged to take lightly whenever he could. I remember Momma-pie's patient and saintly smile, which told the world how much she had borne and how much she was resigned to bear. For if Uncle Andrew's instinct for the outrageous was unfailing, so was Momma-pie's instinct for the vengeance of patient endurance.

One of Uncle Andrew's favorite loitering places was the Rosebud Café just off the courthouse square in Hargrave. The Rosebud sold beer, and my parents did not allow me to go there; it seemed even to me to be no place for children. I never went there alone or with my schoolmates. But in those days I went there often with Uncle Andrew. The Rosebud was owned and run by Miss Iris Flynn, who always had three or four nice young women working for her. It was a good-humored, interesting-smelling place, full of light from the big front windows in the daytime, and at night dim, lit mainly by neon — as I knew from standing on the walk in front and peeking in. Uncle Andrew loved to go there in the lulls that came in the late morning and the middle of the afternoon. Often, then, we would be the only customers. Uncle Andrew would order soft drinks for us, and then he would sit, tilted back in his chair, talking and cutting up with Miss Iris and the other women. They would gather round, or stop in passing, to join in the talk and the carrying on. These interludes were intensely interesting to me, and I devoted a lot of study to them.

One night when I was eating supper with Aunt Judith and Uncle Andrew and Momma-pie at the little table in Aunt Judith's kitchen, I said, "Uncle Andrew, how come you spend so much time talking to those women down at the Rosebud?"

Momma-pie assumed her smile of sweet patience.

Uncle Andrew looked at me and said, "Well, I'll be goddamned!"

But he was already laughing. He either was embarrassed or knew he ought to be, and his embarrassment tickled him. For there I sat, the would-be friend of his bosom, his trusty hired hand, and I had betrayed him.

Burlesquing indignation to disguise whatever she felt — and maybe amused at me too; she could have been — Aunt Judith said, "Well! The next thing I know, Uncle Andrew'll be out in my car with one of those Rosebud girls!"

Uncle Andrew said, "Aw'eah! *Stretched* out in it!"

The big flow of his laughter poured out, and all of us, in our various styles, went bobbing away.

7

My memories of Uncle Andrew are thus an accumulation of little pictures and episodes, isolated from one another, unbegun and unended. They are vividly colored, clear in outline, and spare, as if they belong to an early age of the world when there were not too many details. Each is like the illuminated capital of a page I cannot read, for in my memory there is no tissue of connection or interpretation. As a child, I either was interested or I was not; I either understood or I did not. Mostly, even when I was interested, I did not understand. I had perhaps no inclination to explain my elders to myself. I did not say to myself, "Uncle Andrew is wild," or "Uncle Andrew does not think beforehand," or "Uncle Andrew does whatever he thinks of." Perhaps it was from thinking about him after his death, discovering how much I remembered and how little I knew, that I learned that all human stories in this world contain many lost or unwritten or unreadable or unwritable pages and that the truth about us, though it must exist, though it must lie all around us every day, is mostly hidden from us, like birds' nests in the woods.

For a long time after Uncle Andrew's death, when the phone would ring early in the morning, I would be out of bed and halfway down the stairs before I remembered his absence and felt the day suddenly change around me, withdrawing forever from what it might have been.

That was the way it went for I cannot remember how long. Uncle Andrew was right at the center of the idea I had formed of myself. I was his hand, his boy, his buddy, who was either always going with him or always wanting to go with him. I had wanted to be like him. It had not occurred to me to want to be like anybody else. That he was no longer present was a fact I kept discovering. It puzzled me that I did not cry; perhaps I would have, had I been able to name to myself what I had experienced and what I felt. Uncle Andrew had been a surprising man; often you did not know what he was going to do, and this was because he often did not know what he was going to do himself. But his death was a bigger surprise to me than anything I had seen him do while he was living. That he had been killed on purpose by another man, for a reason that was never adequately explained to me, made his death as much a mystery as it was a surprise. It was therefore a problem to me as much as it was a grief; I thought about it almost incessantly.

For my sake, I suppose, not much was said about Uncle Andrew or his death in my presence. Or maybe it was not for my sake. How easy, after all, would it have been to find the words? What could have been said that would have been adequate or fitting to a calamity so great and so new? The grown-ups' grief, especially my father's, stood silently around the life and death of Uncle Andrew like a wall or a guardian grove. I could no more have spoken of him or asked about the manner of his death than I could have doubted that he was dead.

Somebody told me merely that Carp Harmon had killed Uncle Andrew because Uncle Andrew had failed to cover a well near the lead mine, as he had promised he would do. I asked for no details, accepting the story as the truth, which it partly may have been, though I came to doubt it.

✤

We had an upright piano at our house, and sometimes in the evening my father would play. I had no gift for music, but I liked to hear him and to watch him. He played hymns and popular tunes, sitting very straight at the keyboard, playing with precision and strong rhythm. What I best remember him playing, sometimes singing as he played, was "Bell-Bottom Trousers," a sprightly, morale-boosting song that was popular for a while during the war, and another, a love song, "One Dozen Roses." After Uncle Andrew's death, my father never played the piano again. This was to me the most powerful of all the signs of the change that had come.

He went on with his law practice, of course, but now he also resumed the care of the farms. By then, he had to look after Grandpa Catlett's farm, which we called the Home Place, in addition to the Crayton and Bower Places, because after Uncle Andrew's death Grandpa was less and less able to see to it himself. All this, however great the burden or regrettable the cause, was one of the blessings of his life. Unlike Uncle Andrew, my father had a genuine calling to be a farmer. Farming was his passion, as the law was; in him the two really were inseparable. As a lawyer, he had served mostly farmers. His love of farming and of farming people had led him into the politics of agriculture and a lifelong effort to preserve the economy of the small farms. In my father's assortment of passions—his family, the law, bird hunting, and farming—farming was the fundamental one; from farming he derived the terms and conditions of his being. It was farming that excited him until he could not sleep: "Like a woman!" he would say in his old age, amazed and delighted that it could have moved him so. When he could, he would take a day off from the office to farm: Maybe he would work all day with the cattle or sheep; I remember days too when he would get everybody together to harness and drive for the first time the new teams of two-year-old mules. He made the rounds of the farms every evening, after the office was shut, to see to his livestock, to learn what had been done, to find out what needed doing, or just to drive his car through the fields and look. Or he would stop and sit, and let the world grow still around him. Often he would be out on one of the places, driving and thinking and looking, talking to Jake or Charlie Branch or one of the Brightleafs, before office hours in the morning.

Sometimes he would be late getting back.

"Where's Wheeler?" some would-be client, glancing in at my father's still-empty chair, would ask his secretary.

Miss Julia Vye would raise her hands in a gesture of helplessness and take a noisy little sip of air over the end of her tongue. "Heaven *knows* where! Out somewhere in a *field*, I *suppose!*"

One day as I walked past my father's car, parked on the street in front of his office, I saw a large grasshopper sitting on top of the steering wheel.

By the time my father had owned a car for a year or so, the paint was thoroughly scratched by bushes and briars, and the radiator was choked with seeds.

On Sunday afternoons, after church and dinner, he would be at farming again—he couldn't keep away from it—making the rounds that day with Grandpa, as long as he was able, or with Elton Penn or Nathan Coulter or Henry or me, or sometimes with all of us, Henry and I along to open the gates, to be teased and admonished, to listen. My father would drive slowly and alertly, turning the car abruptly this way or that to show an animal or a field to the best advantage.

When he could not go to the farms himself, he often sent Henry or me or both of us to do some piece of work he wanted done. He almost routinely overtaxed our abilities—as on the day he sent us, when we were still small boys, to separate the bull from the herd of cows on the Crayton Place and drive him to the Home Place; we saw a lot of the country on that trip, for the bull went into every side road and through every open gate he came to. Or else our father sent us to have some pleasure that he was too busy to have himself but that he imagined we could have if only he appointed us to have it and described it suggestively enough: He knew where we could catch a mess of fish or find a covey of birds, and he would tell us not only how to conduct the adventure he had in mind but also how to enjoy it.

Sometimes, later, he would say, as if thinking aloud, how much his interest and enthusiasm had been damaged by Uncle Andrew's death, how that had baffled and delayed him, and I knew that this was so. He regretted bitterly and always the loss of Uncle Andrew, and of that part of his own life that he felt had gone with Uncle Andrew to the grave. But if he was damaged, he was not destroyed; he still had more than half his life to live, and he was a farmer to the end.

Now, looking back after all my years of thinking about the two of them, I cannot help wondering how satisfactorily their partnership might have continued if Uncle Andrew had lived. I know that my father knew that Uncle Andrew was wild—I am pretty sure that he knew the extent of his wildness and what it involved—and yet my father spoke even less of that than of his grief. At the time of Uncle Andrew's death, he and my father had been partners for something like four years. As far as I know, it had gone well enough. Perhaps Uncle Andrew would have proved responsible enough and my father patient enough for their partnership to have endured—who could know? I know only that after Uncle Andrew's death my father suffered not only a lost reality but also a damaged dream. It was a dream bound to sustain damage and to cause pain, and yet he never gave it up, and he passed it on. He dreamed, simply, of a world intact, the family together, the place cared for, and all well.

※

Perhaps without much awareness that he was doing it, or why, he transferred his dream of partnership to Henry and me. Because he needed so much for us to share his interests, his demands on us were often burdening and overburdening, though they taught us much that we needed to know. In spite of his impatience and his sometimes immense exasperation at our shortcomings, he gave us also his love for the ordinary excellences of farming and of life outdoors, and his extraordinary pleasure in them. He could be absorbed and exalted in watching a herd of cattle graze or a red fox crossing a field.

In his eagerness to have us learn and to fill us with experience, he put us into the hands of other teachers. Often, in the summer or on weekends, he would take us with him on his morning rounds and just leave us wherever work was going on.

"Here," he would say to Jake Branch, for often it would be Jake with whom he left us. "Put 'em to work."

And to us he would say, "I want you to work and I want you to mind. Listen to Jake and do what he tells you."

"Jake," he would say, "make 'em do. Make 'em mind."

And Jake would say, "Aw, Mr. Wheeler, don't you worry about *them* boys. *Them* boys is all right. Me and *them* boys get along."

My father would touch the accelerator then, and be on his way.

※

Everything was different at Jake's and Minnie's without Uncle Andrew. It was quieter and plainer than it had been, and it was sad. As elsewhere, little was said about Uncle Andrew in his absence. Even Minnie, who talked easily about anything, would speak his name with care, as if both eager and reluctant to remember him. But it was Minnie who told me the little that I knew for many years about Uncle Andrew's last day.

"Andrew," she said, as if announcing her topic, "he come here that morning to bring Ab home. Ab got his hand cut, it was a bad cut, Andrew taken him to the doctor and then brought him here. And I'm here to tell you, Andrew knowed *then* that something was going to happen to him. He knowed it. He said he felt bad, and could he have a drink of water. I drawed a fresh bucket and give him a drink.

"We about had dinner ready and I said, 'Here, Andrew, set down and eat before you go back.'

"And then he started out the back door; he come in at the front door, bringing Ab in. I said, 'Andrew, it's bad luck to go in one door and out the other.'

"He said, 'It don't matter. It don't make any difference.'

"He went on out the back door. And it weren't but a little while then till he was dead.

"He knowed something was going to happen, I'm atelling you. He knowed it as sure as I'm setting here."

I believed her. Her story seemed to me to show that Uncle Andrew's death had been fated. Whether he entered into the course of his fate by coming in and going out by different doors, as at birth and death, or by some other way, I did not know. But I felt that on the day of his death he had been fated to die, and that he knew it.

Her story made me see him as he had been when he came into the kitchen with death's shadow over him and asked her for a drink of water, and drank, and set down the glass. I heard him say, "It don't matter. It don't make any difference." I can hear him yet. I can see the expression on his face as he says it. The shadow of his death is already on him. He speaks in eternity even as he is speaking in time.

And yet Miss Iris Flynn told me many years later that on that morning, having left Ab with the doctor, Uncle Andrew stuck his head into the door of the Rosebud, gave her a grin, and said, "Hi, babe!"

But of those two glimpses of him on that day, Minnie Branch's is the most powerful. I still raise with myself the question whether it is bad luck to come in by one door and go out by another, which I still associate with that old darkness of fate and calamity. And when I have it on my mind, I still go out by the same door I came in.

᠁

Only once was I ever admitted into the unqualified presence of the family's grief. One night in the late fall of the year of Uncle Andrew's death, I went with my father on his farm rounds after he had left the office for the day. In the dusk of the early evening we stopped to see Grandma and Grandpa Catlett. Grandma asked us and we stayed for supper. This was something my father had always done from time to time, but perhaps he had not done so since Uncle Andrew's death.

Grandma's kitchen was not so harshly utilitarian as Minnie Branch's — it was neater, and the chairs at the table matched — but in its furnishings and aspect it was nonetheless a room mainly to be used. It had no fuss about it, nothing decorative except a calendar. It was a fairly large room, containing in addition to the table and chairs an iron cooking stove, a small coal oil stove sometimes used in hot weather, a wood box, a flour box, a dish cabinet, and by the back door a small wash table with water bucket and pan and a towel made of a flour sack hanging on a nail, the nail protruding through a carefully worked buttonhole. By then, I believe, there would also have been a small refrigerator. The table and chairs were old, covered with many coats of paint, the old coats chipped and cracked beneath the new. I remember from about that time a dishpan that had a leak and was slightly rounded on the bottom; when Grandma set it on the hot stove it was continuously rocked by little explosions of steam. Her fine things consisted of a set of silver teaspoons, a beautiful old painted pitcher, and a cut-glass bowl.

The table, covered with an oilcloth, stood under the windows on the north wall. Cellar, smokehouse, henhouse, and garden were still live institutions in those days. There would have been a crock of fresh milk; Grandma would have fried a stack of corn batter cakes on the griddle; she might have had a baked ham or a hen; the only sign of the war would have been a scarcity of sugar.

While we ate nobody said anything that was not necessary. I was left out of consideration almost as much as I had been in Minnie Branch's kitchen on the day of Uncle Andrew's dance with Mrs. Partlet, and that was unusual.

When the meal was over, we went through the cold hall to the living room and sat down. Grandpa and my father sat on opposite sides of the stove, in which there was a fire. Grandma sat in her little spindle-backed rocker. I sat off to myself by the stand table on which was Grandma's small brown radio. Perhaps, feeling the sorrow in the room, I wanted to turn on the radio, but I did not turn it on. I could not have turned it on, or asked to do so. As several times before in the months since Uncle Andrew's death, I felt as if I had just happened into a world that I had not imagined, in which I found no comfort. I had an obscure feeling that it would be politest to be somewhere else but that there would be no polite way to leave. The grown-ups sat in their chairs for a while, not speaking, and then they started to cry — all three of them. They wept without moving or speaking, each as if alone. And then they ceased. My father and Grandma removed their glasses and wiped away their tears, my father with his handkerchief, my grandmother with a corner of her apron. Grandpa simply raised his right hand and passed his forefinger under his eyes.

No more was said in the car that night as my father and I drove home. I can imagine now that he was searching his mind for something to say to me. He would have been aware of the difficulty for me of what I had witnessed, for he was not unaware of much. Demanding as he could be at times, when sympathy was needed he was generous, and he was good at finding the words. But I cannot imagine what he could have said to ease or mitigate the grief that had shown itself so nakedly to me. I was glad he said nothing.

❧

Carp Harmon was tried and sentenced to two years in the penitentiary. This also was never explained to me, though I knew that my elders resented the lightness of the punishment. I learned of the trial itself only from Jess Brightleaf, who told me that my father had asked him not to attend. If Jess had gone to the trial, then my grandfather would have wanted to go too. The reason for that I understood without being told. Given my grandfather's character, his age, his grief and anger, he would not have considered himself subject to the restraints of the court, and my father did not want him raging there.

Later, after I knew that his sentence had expired, I spent a lot of time wondering what would happen if Carp Harmon gave me a ride while I was hitchhiking. Hitchhiking was another thing Henry and I did that we were absolutely forbidden to do. Our mother had read of many horrible things that had happened to hitchhikers, none of which I thought would happen to me. As I knew from experience, people I did not know who picked me up on the road I traveled, the Port William road, were likely to greet me by asking, "Ain't you one of Wheeler Catlett's boys?" or "I don't reckon you'd be a Catlett, would you?" What I worried about was getting picked up by Carp Harmon. Though I had not knowingly ever seen him, I had no doubt that I would recognize him. And I knew that I would need great courage, greater courage than I was sure I had, to speak the necessary words, which I had rehearsed: "Carp Harmon, you son of a bitch, you killed my uncle." And then perhaps he would pull out his .38 pistol and shoot me?

But he never gave me a ride; as far as I know, I never laid eyes on him in his life.

Another encounter that I grew to expect, as I grew into understanding of what I remembered of Uncle Andrew, was with a first cousin, some strange boy or young man, as I put it to myself, whom I would recognize because he would look something like Uncle Andrew, or even something like me. But if he exists, he has not come forward. As far as I know, I have not laid eyes on him either.

8

Widowhood gave new impetus to Aunt Judith's role as a sufferer. In the eighteen years that remained to her, she needed more sympathy than ever, and now more than ever she was persistent in asking or hinting for it, and was more than ever unappeasable. It was as though every calamity that Momma-pie had forestalled or denied by her masks of superiority had fallen on Aunt Judith, who was as naked to them as a shorn lamb. Whatever her faults, Aunt Judith lacked her mother's arrogance.

Yet as her afflictions grew she seemed to become increasingly self-concerned. Her sufferings finally were not at all conditioned by the understanding that others also suffered; she suffered in an almost pristine innocence, as if she were the world's unique sufferer and the world waited curiously to hear of her pains. She was so prompt and extravagent in pitying herself that she drove away all competitors.

She called Grandma Catlett on every anniversary of Uncle Andrew's birth and death, and on every other anniversary or holiday that reminded her of her loss and her suffering. She kept this up year after year, speaking of "our Andrew." Grandma said that she was grateful for these attentions, but they cannot have been easy for her.

Nor was Aunt Judith an easy burden for my father, who, in Uncle Andrew's absence, became her adviser and protector. He fulfilled his duties faithfully, but without, I think, ever having the satisfaction of feeling that she was satisfied.

When Momma-pie died, my father had the duty, among others, of taking Aunt Judith to the undertaker's to pick out a coffin. He got me to go along, but both of us together were as unequal to the occasion as he would have been alone. We knew that Aunt Judith had been dependent on Momma-pie for many things. We knew that Momma-pie's death would leave Aunt Judith much lonelier than before. But our sympathy was so much a surplus as to be hardly noticeable.

Handkerchief in hand, chin quivering, Aunt Judith said many times that she was going to be awfully lonely now. Many times she said she did not know what she was going to do. She gazed lingeringly into every one of the coffins, of which there was a roomful, and every one of them reminded her of her loss and renewed her grief. Every one of the coffins had something about it that Momma-pie would have liked, and at these reminders of Momma-pie's tastes and preferences Aunt Judith's voice would become a whisper and she would dab at her eyes. She was using her grief to invite sympathy, and in doing so falsified her grief, and in falsifying her grief made it impossible to sympathize with her. And she compounded the difficulty by the innocence of perfect self-deception; she had, I feel sure, no idea what she was doing. And what was one to say? I could find in myself not the least aptitude for the occasion. I longed to exchange places with the wallpaper or the rug. My father, having assured Aunt Judith that he would do all he could for her, had almost as little to say as I did. She placed and left us in our embarrassment as she would have seated us at a table.

For some years she worked as a typist in one of the offices in Hargrave. Later, she contracted glaucoma and became virtually blind. She made her way about the town then truly alone, avoided under cover of her blindness by people who could no longer bear her importunities for sympathy and her endless recitation of her ills.

My last clear, unshakable memory of her is from the summer of 1949, when I was fifteen. One afternoon as I was walking in front of the courthouse, I called out to one of my friends, and in the same instant looked across the street and saw Aunt Judith. She had recognized my voice, and she turned to stare sightlessly toward me. I did not want to go to her; I was just empty of the willingness to do so. I went on as I intended to go, pretending under her following blind gaze that it was not my voice that she had heard and that I was not myself.

For want of compassion—aware that I would inevitably fail to be compassionate enough, but also for want of enough compassion—I denied that I was who I was, and so made myself less than I was. This was my first conscious experience of a shame that was irremediable and hopeless—a shame, as I now suppose, that Uncle Andrew may have met in himself, in her presence, many a time.

This surely was the punishment that she dealt out, wittingly or not, willingly or not, to him and to the rest of us. And if at times in the past I could abandon her to the self-martyrdom of the self-absorbed, and though I see now better than then how impossible she was, still I am sorry. For I can no longer forget that loss and illness and trouble, however a person may exploit them, cannot be exploited without being suffered. Aunt Judith exploited them and suffered them, and suffered her exploitation of them. She suffered and she was alone.

And so she is inescapable. In my mind I will always see her standing there in the street, her head tilted stiffly up, hopelessly hoping for some earthly pity greater than her pity for herself.

9

The house that Uncle Andrew seemed most to be gone from was not, for me, the one where he had lived in rented rooms with Aunt Judith and Momma-pie. Nor was it my own house at Hargrave, or Jake and Minnie's at the Crayton Place. Where I most often met his absence and was obliged to deal with it was at Grandma and Grandpa Catlett's.

Grandpa had been born in an earlier house on that site, the last of five children, about a year before the end of the Civil War. That house burned when he was six, and the present house was built on the old foundation. In the second winter after Uncle Andrew's death, Grandpa took sick, went to bed, and did not get up again.

All his life he had gone to the barn at bedtime to see to his animals and make sure that all was well. That winter, staying at night with Grandpa, my father went to the barn at bedtime and returned to say that all was well. "And then," my father said, "he would be pleased."

"The day after I die," Grandpa told my father, "get up and go to work." He died where he was born, in the same corner of the same room, though in a different house. And on a raw day in the late winter we carried him, dressed up, to Port William and left him there in the hill under the falling rain.

The year and a half and a little more between the day of Uncle Andrew's death and the day of Grandpa's funeral seems to me now to have been a time of ending, not just of lives but of a kind of life and a kind of world. I did not recognize that ending as consciously then as I do now, but I felt its shadow. Uncle Andrew had not belonged to the older life; though he had grown up in it, he had lived away from it. He belonged to the self-consciously larger life that came into being with the First World War, and that was now rapidly establishing itself by means of another war, industrial machinery, and electric wires. But though that new world was undeniably present on the roads, the life of our fields still depended on the bodily strength and skill of people and horses and mules. In the minds of my grandfather and Dick Watson, the Brightleafs, and the Branches, the fundamental realities and interests and pleasures were the same as they had been in the minds of the people who had worked in the same fields before the Civil War.

The first death after Uncle Andrew's had been Dick Watson's, and Dick, like my grandfather, belonged to that older world. That the two of them belonged also to two different and in some ways opposite races did not keep them from belonging in common to a kind of humanity. They were farming people. What distinguished them from ever-enlarging numbers of people in succeeding generations was that they had never thought of being anything else. This gave them a kind of integrity and a kind of concentration. They did their work with undivided minds, intent upon its demands and pleasures, reconciled to its hardships, not complaining, never believing that they might have been doing something better.

Dick and Aunt Sarah Jane's two-room house at the edge of the woods, down the hill from the barns, was a part of the Home Place, but it was also a place unto itself, with its own garden and henhouse and woodpile. Aunt Sarah Jane did not work "out." She kept house and gardened and cared for a small flock of chickens and foraged in the fields and woods and sewed and mended and read her Bible. In the mornings and the evenings and in odd times spared from the farmwork, Dick kept their house supplied with water and milk, meat and firewood. I remember their pleasure in all the items of their small abundance: buckets of milk from Dick's cow, cured joints and middlings from their hogs, vegetables from Aunt Sarah Jane's garden, the herbs and greens and mushrooms she gathered on her walks.

In those years when I could not be with Uncle Andrew, I loved almost as much to be with Dick, though the two of them could hardly have been less alike. Dick was as gentle and quiet as Uncle Andrew was brash and uproarious. And whereas Uncle Andrew's great aim in life was to "get out among 'em," Dick, when I knew him, anyhow, was mostly content to stay put. With Uncle Andrew, you were always on a trajectory that was going to take you back to the road and on to someplace else. With Dick, when he wasn't behind a team or on horseback, you traveled on foot, going not away but deeper in. Dick could sit still. He could sit on his rock doorstep after supper, smoke his pipe, and talk slowly and thoughtfully until bedtime. In my memories of Uncle Andrew, I am often behind him or off to the side, watching him, feeding my curiosity as to what manner of man he was. In my memories of Dick Watson, I am often beside him, holding his hand. From Dick I learned that the countryside was inhabited not just by things we ordinarily see but also by things we ordinarily do not see— such as foxes. That it was haunted by old memories I already knew.

Foxhunting with Dick, he on my grandfather's mare and I on Beauty the pony, I first came into the presence of the countryside at night, and learned to think of it as the hunters knew it, and learned there were foxes abroad in it who knew it as no human ever would. There would be an occasional dog fox, Dick said, who would venture up almost to the yard fence to invite the hounds to run, and who, when the hounds accepted the challenge, knew how to baffle them by running in a creek or along the top of a rock fence. I had from Dick a vision of a brilliant fox running gaily through the dark over the ridges and along the hollows, followed by hounds in beautiful outcry, and this to me was a sort of doctrineless mystery and grace.

But what I remember most, and most gratefully, is Dick's own presence, for he was a man fully present in the place and its yearly round of work that connected hayfield and grainfield and feed barn and hog lot, woods and woodpile and the wood box behind the kitchen stove, well and water trough. When the work was to be done, he was there to do it. He did it well and without haste; when it was done he took his ease and did not complain. Years later, when I was looking for the way home, his was one of the minds that guided me.

After he and then Grandpa were dead, the farm, in spite of my father's long caring for it, lacked a coherence that it had had before. It needed not just attention and work but lives that made it a world and lived from it.

For several years after those deaths, I stayed with Grandma for months at a time. She started coming to Hargrave to spend the winters in a room at the Broadfield Hotel. And then on a Saturday morning in March or April, with spring bright in the air, Elton Penn would come with his truck, and we would load Grandma's spool bed, her comfortable rocker, her clothes and linens, and take her home.

I would move in then to stay with her until she returned to town late the following fall. For me, this was freedom, more freedom probably than I was entitled to, but not more than I wanted and even needed. At Grandma's, I was the man of the house. I had as my own room the little hallway behind Grandma's bedroom, and I had, as it seemed to me, the whole country to range in, on foot or horseback, beyond sight or call of any grown-up. For grown-up company, when I wanted it, I had Grandma, and after 1945 Elton and Mary Penn on the Beechum Place, and Jess and Rufus Brightleaf and their wives. For a playmate, I had Fred Brightleaf. When my father took me or sent me to work for Jake Branch, I had the company of that large and various household. Hargrave, when I returned to it, took some getting used to. I decided to stay out of it if I could.

To get to school, I rode the bus or hitchhiked down to Hargrave in the morning and back again in the afternoon. I attended school by requirement only. I did not think of it when I was not in it. I did not establish a great reputation as a student.

Once Grandma and I had moved in, we revived the old house around us. I thought it a great adventure to build a fire again in the kitchen range and to help Grandma get together the makings of our first meal. On the colder mornings we would get up and hurry down to the kitchen to renew the fire. Charmed by the elemental pleasure of needing to be warm and then getting warm, I watched the day grow bright outside the windows while Grandma cooked our breakfast. As we ate, the sun came up beyond the still-living oak snag at the corner of the woods.

This was a homecoming for me as much as for Grandma. I had lived there with my parents during my first two years. I had come newborn to that house. It was the first house of my memory and consciousness. Sleeping there in my crib beside my parents' bed, I had dreamed the sounds of the wind that drew its long breaths over the house at night. And I remembered waking there as if to a world entirely new, to see the sun shining on the wet grass and the white barns.

By the time I was born into it, the history of that place had become old. The sign of its age was much forgetfulness. Much had happened to us there that we did not remember. We had suffered and rejoiced there more than we knew. I acquired experiences there that never had happened to me at all. All my life I have recalled a sort of dream image of a man putting on his coat at the back door, speaking over his shoulder to a woman inside the house. A freed slave going away? One of our family going west? Or simply somebody going to the field? I cannot see his face; I do not know.

I had known, it seemed to me always, that when Grandpa was "just a little bit of a baby laying up yonder in the bed," some soldiers had come at night and taken his father. They were a small band of Union horsemen who had come to "recruit" my great-grandfather, who would have been in his early forties at the time. They did this, I suppose, with a pleasant sense of justice, because he owned a few slaves and for that and other reasons would not have been sympathetic to their cause. Forcing him to mount behind one of them, they carried him to their encampment on the top of the next hill. Still in her nightgown and barefooted, my great-grandmother, Lizzie, followed them. By force of argument or character or both, she "made them give him back." According to the story as I heard it, Lizzie "ran after them," and so in my mind, as if from my own birth, I have had the image of that distraught and determined woman running up the dark road.

And I have had in mind always the fire that burned the old house when Grandpa was six. It is a pod of fierce light that opens greatly in the dark. In that light Grandpa is a small boy suddenly filled with terrible knowledge. He stands holding his saddle, his most precious possession, which he has retrieved from under his bed. They bring to him a small Negro girl, the cook's daughter, a year younger than he. She is hysterical, wanting to run back into the burning house. And they tell him, "Hold her! Hold her tight!" And he holds her, while the grown-ups continue their effort to save things from the house, and then finally give up and watch it burn.

The new house had grown old too by the time I knew it, and had about it memories and reminders and intimations of unremembered things. The house itself was tall and finely outlined. Its high-ceilinged rooms, cool in summer, were lovely when filled with morning light. But its furnishings were meager and rather graceless. The best room, the parlor, in which we sat only on the most special occasions, contained an upright piano with a stool, a matching sofa and easy chair covered with rose and beige brocade, a glass-fronted bookcase, a small table, and two or three more chairs, not necessarily comfortable. The other rather formal room was the dining room, likewise seldom used. It was a north room, cool in summer, cold in winter, heated, like the parlor, only by a fireplace. I liked to go into that room for its strangeness and its cold smells of cloves and brown sugar.

The kitchen, living room, and three bedrooms upstairs — the rooms that were to varying degrees lived in — were furnished with not much of an eye for decoration or harmony. The furniture was inherited or haphazardly bought or come by; nearly all of it was old and well worn, some of it damaged or much repaired. The rugs were threadbare in spots, and where the travel was heaviest the finish was worn off the kitchen linoleum. It was a house that for a long time had been occupied by people struggling to hold themselves in place, who had not had much time for comfort or the means for luxuries. I understood this only much later; then it was merely familiar. The house had had a telephone for a good many years and electricity for four or five, but nothing else had changed, and it seemed somehow surprised by these amenities. It still had no running water. We used the privy down in a corner of the backyard, and carried water in buckets from the well.

There were a few framed photographs on the living room wall — pictures of Uncle Andrew and my father, and of us children. There was also a small tintype of Grandpa when he was a young boy; his mother had had to whip him, he said, to make him sit still for it. Upstairs there were larger photographic portraits of Uncle Andrew and my father as children, and of my great-grandfathers Catlett and Wheeler. Grandma's decorations consisted mainly of a few crocheted doilies and table scarves. Her yearning for nice things was revealed by her attachment to ornamented candy boxes with hinged lids; the few of these that she had received she kept and filled with photographs, letters, and the pretty greeting cards that came on holidays. The most beautiful thing in the house, I thought, was a sampler made by my mother. I read it often, fascinated by the close rhymes. It said:

HOURS FLY
FLOWERS DIE
NEW DAYS
NEW WAYS
PASS BY
LOVE STAYS

Between us, Grandma and I carried on the best we could the old kitchen economy of milk cow and hen flock and garden. I helped her care for the hens, and I did the milking and sometimes the churning.

To amuse myself while I milked the cows I would sometimes take aim at the flies that lit on the rim of the bucket and squirt them down into the foam. Grandma, seeing them in the strainer, would say, "Lord, the *flies*! Did anybody ever *see* the like!"

When I churned, sitting on the back porch with the stone churn between my knees, I could make buttermilk fly up through the dasher hole and hit the ceiling. And then Grandma would say, "Well, if you ain't the limit!"

When I would catch a nice mess of little sunfish at the pond, or a turtle, or anything wild and good to eat, she would say, "Well, *did* you ever!"

One bright day after rain, when I had waded along the risen branch picking raspberries with Elton Penn, who wore a pair of gum boots and was going directly ahead as usual, Grandma ignored the cap full of berries I held out to her and looked at my sopping shoes and pants legs. "Andy Catlett, I reckon you haven't got a lick of sense!"

I loved to stay with her, partly because she spoiled me, partly because she left me pretty free to live the life available in that place, which was the life I wanted. In the long summer mornings and afternoons I went alone on foot or horseback among the fields and woods and ponds and streams. Or I swam or quested about with Fred Brightleaf. Or I worked, if I could and if allowed, with the Brightleafs or Elton Penn or Jake Branch.

At mealtimes, and while we went about our chores, and at night,

Grandma and I talked. Mainly she talked; I questioned and listened. She talked of things that had happened and of things that had been said, things that she remembered and things that she remembered that other people had remembered. At night it was best. After the supper dishes were put away, the long light and heat of the day now past, we would darken the house and go out to sit on the front porch. Or if the breeze was better out in the yard we would carry chairs out and sit at the foot of a big old cedar tree that stood there then. While the lightning bugs carried their little winking lamps up out of the grass, and the katydids sang in the late summer foliage, and heat lightning shimmered on the horizon, we sat invisible to each other, just two voices talking, until bedtime.

She told of the roads and distances of the old days, of the time when the little patch of woods by Dick Watson's house had been part of a bigger woods that went on and on. She told of slavery times, when my great-grandmother, resting after dinner in the room over the kitchen, heard Molly, the cook, tell the cat, "Old Lizzie's asleep now, and I'm going to beat the hell out of you." She told of the end of slavery, when all the slaves went away, and Molly returned and was sent away. "You have your freedom now," Lizzie told her, "and you must go."

She told and retold, because I wanted to hear, of the night the soldiers came, and of the burning house.

She talked of Grandpa. There had been serious estrangements and difficulties between them, for both of them were strong-willed people, and they had not always willed the same things. But now in his absence that we both felt, she took pleasure in remembering him in his youth and his pride. She said, "He was the finest-looking man on the back of a horse that ever I saw." She said he was a beautiful whistler. She had loved to hear him, off somewhere in the distance, calling his cattle. She knew what hard times and failures and disappointments had cost him, and she sorrowed for him as she sorrowed for herself when she had been young and proud, paying the same costs. There had been times when they had barely made it.

As a young wife she had lived with her mother-in-law, about whom I never heard her complain, and she remembered much that Lizzie had remembered: what the cook had said to the cat, for example, or an exchange of letters between Lizzie and her brother, James. James,

Grandma said, was elected to the state legislature. When he was to be sworn in, he invited Lizzie to attend the ceremony. She wrote back, "I have nothing suitable to wear." And James replied, "Wear the simplest thing you have, and let your manners correspond."

One of my favorite people in Grandma's stories was Grandpa's older brother, Will, indolent and vagrant, careless and fearless, a comedian drunk or sober, a disappointment and an aggravation to everybody, and yet dear.

"Will," Grandma asked him once, "were you ever in love with Sally Skaggs?"

"Yes, Dorie," he said, "I loved her a little once."

It was Uncle Will who cut off Uncle Andrew's long golden curls "to turn him into a boy," and broke Grandma's heart.

She told also, troubled and yet amused, of her own younger brother, Leonidas, whom we all called "Uncle Peach," who would get drunk and say to her, "Sing 'Yellow Rose o' Texas' to me, madam."

And it was Uncle Peach who had allowed Uncle Andrew to fall into the fire when he had just begun to walk, leaving what I thought a most attractive set of small scars across the backs of the fingers of Uncle Andrew's right hand.

Grandma recalled a Negro farmhand, Uncle Mint Wade, who argued, "You will read in the Bible whereupon it say, 'The bottom rail shall be the rider.'"

And she remembered Uncle Eb Markman, who pronounced, "The world is squar' and got four cawners to it."

From her reading she had culled a few phrases that she liked to repeat. It pleased her to speak of sleep as "nature's sweet restorer." Her speech had touches of self-conscious elegance that she used in tribute. Of dancing she would say, "It's a lovely thing, stepping to the music."

Our most frequent and fearful topic was the weather. Both of us were afraid of storms, which seemed to be uncommonly frequent in those days. Grandma would tell about storms that she remembered, and we would discuss the problem of where to be safe in case of a windstorm.

Before a thunderstorm, she would put a pillow over the telephone, theorizing that the feathers made good insulation and would prevent the lightning from coming into the house along the wire. And having affixed the pillow to the wall so that it covered the phone, she would always quote Uncle Will: "I believed that too, Dorie, till I saw lightning strike a goose."

When a cold spell would come late in the spring, causing us to feel that some fundamental disorder was at hand, she would quote from a source I have never found: "The time will come when we'll not know the winter from the summer but by the budding of the trees." And though that time has never come, I believed then that it would come, and I believe it still.

Like many country people of her time, she did not have a very secure belief in progress. She believed that hard times did not go away forever, but returned. She had known hard times, and she did not forget them. There had been a winter, when my father was about seven years old, when Grandpa's tobacco crop had not brought enough to pay the commission on its own sale. Grandma could not have forgotten that if she had lived a thousand years. My father's lifelong devotion to the cause of the small farmers of our part of the country dates from that memory, and it holds its power still over Henry and me.

It seemed to have gone by Uncle Andrew without touching him. Uncle Andrew was sometimes burdened and was sometimes a burden to himself, but he also had the gift of taking things lightly. Grandma would quote, with disapproval and with a laugh, his reply to Grandpa, who was worrying about a field infested with wild onions: "The cows'll eat 'em, and I don't have to sleep with the cows."

Grandma was thirteen when her mother died. Her father never remarried. She and her sisters grew up keeping house for themselves and their father and attempting with less than success to give a proper upbringing to Uncle Peach. For Grandma and her sisters, somehow, a mark of respectability and even gentility had been set. They cherished the schooling they got from the Bird's Branch School and *McGuffey's Eclectic Readers,* one through eight. All her life Grandma had struggled and aspired, and her ambition had been confronted and affronted at every turn by the likes of Uncle Will and Uncle Peach and Uncle Andrew, too wayward to be approved, too close and dear to be denied.

❧

Uncle Andrew and Uncle Will and Uncle Peach passed and returned in her thoughts and her talk like orbiting planets. They divided her mind; they troubled her without end. She could see plainly what a relief it would have been if she could have talked some sense into their heads and straightened them out. It would have been a relief too if she could have waved them away and forgotten them. In fact, she could do neither. They were incorrigible, and they were her own. In their various ways and styles, they had worried and vexed and grieved her "nearly into the grave," as she would sometimes say. And they also charmed and amused and moved her. They were not correctable because of the way they were; they were not dismissable because of the way she was. She loved them not even in spite of the way they were, but just because she did. With them she enacted, as many mothers have done, and many fathers too, the parable of the lost sheep, who is to be sought and brought back without end, brought back into mind and into love without end, death no deterrent, futility no bar.

And so she suffered. She looked upon the human condition, I think, as not satisfactory—as unacceptable, notwithstanding that we are in it whether we accept it or not. She was a professed Christian and loved her little weatherboarded church, but I think that it was not easy, and may have been impossible, for her to make peace with our experience of mortality and error, of owning what we cannot correct or save, of losing what we love.

Grandma was fiercely, fiercely loyal to her own, and just as fiercely exclusive in electing her own. Within the small circle of her own, she was capable of profound charity; outside it, she could be relentless and unforgiving. And the boundary was not impermeable. Sometimes Uncle Andrew, for one, had been safely inside it, and sometimes he had been outside. When you were outside, as I knew from my own experience, her anger was direct and her tongue sharp.

Her term of execration was "Hmh!" which she could deliver as concussively as a blow and in tones varying from polite disbelief (for the benefit of guests) to absolute rejection. Her term of contempt was "Psht!" With it she could slice you off like the top of a radish.

Uncle Andrew had crossed the boundary into and out of her good graces many times. The nights of those years after his death, as we sat and talked, she was forever picking apart the divergent strands of her feeling for him. She would be pleased or amused or appalled, or amused and appalled both at once. And always she grieved.

When he was little, with that head covered with golden curls that she could not forget, he was beautiful. He could sing like an angel. And yet he was difficult and mischievous and never still. From the womb, virtually, he lived always a little beyond anyone's anticipation. Even before he could walk, she would have to restrain him by pinning his dresstail under the leg of the bed. He had hardly learned to walk when he flung her good blue pitcher onto the flagstones by the porch step. When he was old enough to receive as a gift his own little hatchet, he chopped one of the rungs out of the banister. She would say regretfully and a little proudly that after he started to school he had become a good fighter. Proudly and a little doubtfully she would say that there never had been anything like the way he could dance.

When he was ready for college, Grandma and Grandpa sent him to the University of Kentucky in a blue blazer—as handsome a young man, they thought, as they had ever laid eyes on—and to do so they spent all they had; Grandpa went without underwear that winter. When he went to Lexington to see his son, he looked everywhere and could not find him, for Uncle Andrew's adventures had begun. His fame as a dancer apparently began during his brief stay at the university.

Grandpa failed in Uncle Andrew, as he succeeded in my father, and it was a bitter failure. Except for the energy that both of them possessed in abundance, Grandpa and Uncle Andrew were as unlike as a tree and a bird. Grandpa could not tolerate, he could not understand, Uncle Andrew's waste of daylight. For him, Andrew was the name of whatever was careless. "Sit up!" he used to say to me as I went by on the pony. "You ride like your Uncle Andrew." It was not that Uncle Andrew rode badly but that he rode carelessly, his mind elsewhere, and Grandpa believed, and said, that "a man ought to keep his mind on his business"—he meant busy-ness, whatever you were doing. Uncle Andrew was Grandma's failure too, of course. It was a mutual property, that failure; it bound them in mutual suffering and even mutual sympathy, and yet I think it stood between them like a heap of thorns. I imagine that their ways of regret were different. Perhaps Grandpa only saw what had happened and named it and bore it, whereas Grandma saw before her always the beautiful child and forgave and hoped. Perhaps. I do not know.

When Grandma and I looked through her collection of photographs that had come with letters from various family members, we would come to a picture of several men in army uniforms squatting in a circle, shooting craps. One of them unmistakably was Uncle Andrew, who had sent the picture, and she would always say "Hmh!" and she would laugh. The laugh seemed both to acknowledge her embarrassment and confess her delight. She delighted in him though he had grieved her nearly into the grave.

He was on her mind forever, and as the evening wore on toward bedtime she would begin again to grieve for him. And always as we approached her grief, we were divided. My loss was nothing like hers. My loss had occurred within the terms of my childhood; it was answered, beyond anything I felt or willed, by my youth and unbidden happiness and all the time I had to live. Her loss would be unrelieved to the end of her life, never mind that she would live on until I was grown and married; her loss was what she had lived to at last and would not live beyond. I could feel that she had come to loss beyond life, unfathomable and inconsolable, as dimensionless as the dark that surrounded the old house and filled it as we talked.

He was on my mind forever too, as I now see. But I was a child; for me, every day was new. I lived beyond my loss even as I suffered it, and without any particular sympathy for myself. And what I have grown into is not sympathy for myself as I was but sympathy for Grandma and Grandpa as they were. I see how time had brought them, once, their years of strength and hope, energy to look forward and build and dream, as we must; and I see how Uncle Andrew took all they had vested in him, their precious one life and time given over in helpless love and hope into the one life and time that he possessed, and how he carried it away on the high flood of his recklessness, his willingness to do whatever he thought of.

I see now what perhaps I have known for a long time that I would see, if I looked: He was a child who wanted only to be free, as I myself had been free back at the pond that afternoon of his death. He was a big, supremely willful child whom Grandma and Grandpa and Aunt Judith could not confine, and who could be balked by no requirement or demand. And yet, hating confinement, he had been confined — in a hapless marriage, in bad jobs, sometimes in self-reproach, and finally in a grave with which he had made no terms. He had been confined because he had confined himself, as only he could have done, because he was the way he was and would not change, or could not. It was knowledge of his confinement, I think, that so surrounded us with pain and made us grieve so long.

When bedtime came, I would go up the stairs first and get into my bed in the little back hall, leaving the door open to the room where Grandma slept. I would hear her stirring in the rooms below, setting things to rights, making sure she had forgotten nothing. Assuming perhaps that I was asleep, she would have begun to talk aloud to herself. "Mm-*hmh!*" she would say as she shut a door or lowered a sash, "Mm-*hmh!*" as she turned off the lights.

And then I would hear her coming slowly up the stairs, the banister creaking under her hand as though now, alone with her thoughts, she bore the whole accumulated weight of time and loss. As she came up, she would be saying to herself always the same thing: "Oh, my poor boy! Oh, my poor, poor boy!"

I would hear her muttering still as she went about her room, preparing for bed: "May God have mercy on my poor boy!"

And then it would be dark. And then it would be morning.

10

The time had to come, of course, when what I knew no longer satisfied me. I had been told almost nothing about the circumstances of Uncle Andrew's murder, I had asked nothing, and yet I wanted to know. That death had remained in the forefront of my mind, as I knew it had in my grandmother's and my father's and Aunt Judith's. I knew too that for other people it had receded and diminished as it had mingled with other concerns. I could not have asked those whom my questions would have pained the most. With others, the subject did not come up. I did not want my curiosity about it to be known.

But finally when I was maybe in my last year of high school, I became conscious that there were such things as court records. The county court clerk at that time was Charlie Hardy, as dear a friend, I suppose, as my father had; they bird-hunted together. I made up my mind to ask Mr. Hardy to show me the records of Carp Harmon's trial, expecting to see transcripts of the lawyers' arguments and the testimony of witnesses; I imagined that there would be a great pile of papers that I could sit down somewhere and read, and at last know everything I wanted to know.

I watched for a time when Mr. Hardy was in his office alone. I did not want anybody but him to hear my request. Above all, I did not want my father to know what I was doing. What I intended to do was unbandage a wound. It was in part my own wound, but I felt it was my father's more than mine, and maybe I had no right to know more than he had told me.

Though I was determined to see those papers, I was also more than a little ashamed.

"Son, I'll show you," Mr. Hardy said when I finally walked in and asked him. "I'll show you what there is, I'll *show* you, son, but there ain't much."

Already I was sorry I had come, for I saw that he knew exactly what I wanted and that he too was thinking of my father. Spitting fragments of tobacco bitten from the cold stump of his cigar, he climbed a ladder up a large wall of file boxes ranked on shelves, selected one of the boxes, and brought it to me.

"See," he said, "there's not a hell of a lot here that would be of interest to you, son." He showed me the warrant for Carp Harmon's arrest, his indictment, several pleadings, all technical documents no more informative than they were required to be.

"I thought there would be a record of what was said at the trial."

"Naw, son," he said. "Nawsir, son, no such record was ever made. What was said at that trial is a long time gone."

He explained that there had been no appeal. There would have been a transcript only if there had been an appeal. By then I was relieved that there was no record. Mr. Hardy was putting the papers back into their box. "Nawsir, son, that record you want to see, it never did exist." He removed the cigar from his mouth, spat toward the wastebasket, and then looked at me. "Son," he said, "I'm sorry."

And still we both were embarrassed, for even though the record I sought did not exist, the fact remained that Charlie Hardy knew what had happened at that trial. I knew he could imagine my saying, "Well, Mr. Hardy, why don't you *tell* me what happened?" And I knew—I know much more certainly now—that he would have given years off his life to be spared the question.

"Well, thank you, Mr. Hardy," I said.

"Any time, son," he said. "Any time." He waved to me with the hand holding the cigar as if I were already out of the building and across the street. "By God, son, come back! *Any* time!"

But as time went on I did learn some things. Things that I did not know to ask for came to me on their own.

One day after the ewes were sheared, when Elton Penn and Henry and

I hauled the bagged wool to market, we ran into Yeager Stump. Something was said about dancing. Maybe Elton mentioned that Henry and I were going to a dance, or had been to one; maybe he was complaining, as he sometimes did, joking, but only half joking, that when we danced late into the night we were no account in the daytime. Whatever was said, it reminded Mr. Stump of Uncle Andrew.

"Boys," he said, and there was laughter in his eyes though he did not laugh aloud, "I've seen your uncle Andrew too drunk to walk, but I never saw him too drunk to dance."

Later it was Mr. Stump, leaning to talk to me through a car window, his eyes filled with that same quiet, reminiscent, almost tender unuttered laughter, who told me two little bits of Uncle Andrew's poetry. "Your uncle Andrew said that when he was with a woman and that old extremity came to him, every hair in his bee-hind was a jew's harp playing a different tune." Mr. Stump's voice recovered exactly Uncle Andrew's jazzy intonation. "He said a big covey of quail flew out his bunghole one bird at a time."

And then Mr. Stump did laugh aloud, briefly. He clapped his hand onto the metal windowsill and straightened up. "Well, he was something. There never was another one like him."

When I went away to Lexington to the university, forty years after Uncle Andrew's failed expedition there, I continued my checking account at the Independent Farmers Bank at Port William. A number of times when I wrote out a check for a woman salesclerk, the lady would look at my signature and the name of the town, and she would say — it was invariably the same sentence — "I knew an Andrew Catlett once."

"He was my uncle," I would say.

And then she would say, "He was *such* a dancer!" Or "Oh, *how* that man could dance!" Or "I just *loved* to dance with him! He was so handsome."

They always spoke of him as a dancer. They always smiled in remembering him. Speaking of him, they always sounded younger than they were, and a little dreamy.

One day in Lexington I cashed a check at Scoop Rawl's Ice Cream Parlor. Scoop himself was at the cash register. He looked at my signature. "Andrew Catlett," he said. "Port William. I knew an Andrew Catlett from down there."

"Yessir," I said. "He was my uncle."

He looked at me over his glasses. "Your uncle. God almighty, we had some times!"

I said, "Yessir," hoping he would say more, and he did, a little. He had known Uncle Andrew, apparently, not during his brief visit to Lexington as a student, but after his marriage, when he was traveling for a distillery.

"Andrew had a girl he called Sweetie Pie. He'd squall for her when he was drunk and you could hear him half a mile: 'Sweetie *Pie!*'"

I *knew* how he sounded. I could hear that raucous mating call rising in the midst of the late-night fracas and hilarity of some Lexington blind tiger as Uncle Andrew hooked cute little Sweetie Pie with his right arm and pulled her into his lap. During my college years also I encountered a woman who had lived near us in Hargrave when I was a child. She had been beautiful when she was young and had been married to an old man. Uncle Andrew, she told me, laughing, had said to her, "When that old son of a bitch is dead, I'm going to stomp on his grave until he's in there good and tight, and then I'm going to get straight into bed with you."

She told me too of the midnight when Uncle Andrew and his cronies in their mating plumage, transcendently drunk, burst into Momma-pie's bedroom, and Uncle Andrew snapped on the light. "Wake up, Momma-pie! We've bred all the women, cows, yo sheep, mares, and mare mules — and now, by God, we're going to breed you!"

In spite of Yeager Stump's later claim that they did whatever they thought of, I do not believe that this actually happened; if it had, Uncle Andrew's moments of retrospective self-knowledge and regret would have forbidden him to talk about it, but it was a story that was known because he had told it.

I can imagine a night of hilarity, Uncle Andrew and Buster Simms and Yeager Stump out among 'em, women and whiskey on hand, Uncle Andrew talking, the others laughing and egging him on. He is conjuring up the most outrageous scene he can think of: he and his buddies crowding into that chastely fragrant room like a nightmare, the sudden light revealing Momma-pie in her nightcap, sans teeth, sitting up in bed, clutching the bedclothes to her bosom. I can imagine the tale repeated and improved at every opportunity as if it had actually happened, the work of alcoholic incandescence and a refined sense of impropriety.

But I know too that Mr. Stump was right: A lot of the things they thought of, they did. Their taste in women ran simply to the available; their pleasures were restricted only by the possible. In his times of breaking out, which apparently were the times he lived for, Uncle Andrew granted an uncomplicated obedience to impulses that men of faith and loyalty like my father struggle against all their lives. Men who obey those impulses surely invite their own destruction, and I think there were moments when Uncle Andrew knew this.

But obviously not all are destroyed. Yeager Stump, for one, enjoyed life far beyond the conventional three score years and ten. Even at the end, when he was housebound, he continued to enjoy life. Miss Iris Flynn, devoted as always, kept him supplied with good bourbon. On one of her visits, she handed him the anticipated bottle and exclaimed about its lately increased cost. "Yes," said Mr. Stump, "maybe they'll finally charge what it's worth."

Whether or not Uncle Andrew invited the destruction he in fact received is at least a disturbed question, and perhaps an unanswerable one. But I did not even know it was a question until one day — I was grown by then — I said point-blank to Elton Penn: "Why did Carp Harmon kill Uncle Andrew?"

Probably Elton was no more comfortable with my curiosity than Mr. Hardy had been, but he gave me a straight answer. "Well, the way I heard it, your Uncle Andrew propositioned Harmon's daughter there in the store where the ones that were tearing down those buildings would go for lunch."

It was not as though Elton and I were two people merely interested in the pursuit of truth; we both knew the hardship that that story would have presented to my family. We did not pursue the subject further, partly because of the pain that surrounded it, partly because I thought the explanation credible and had no more questions to ask. I believed that if he had thought of doing so, Uncle Andrew would have propositioned Carp Harmon's daughter in the store, devil take the witnesses. He would have done it because he thought of doing it and because he enjoyed the outrageousness of it and because he relished the self-abandonment of it. From there, I supposed, the story had gone on to its conclusion according to the logic of anger.

The year following my grandmother Catlett's death, I returned with my wife and baby daughter to live through the summer in the old house. Grandma's things were still there, put away in their places, just as she had left them, and it fell to me to dispose of them. Because she had known no extravagance in her life, she had saved everything salvageable: string, pieces of cloth, buttons and buckles, canceled checks and notes, bits of paper covered with now meaningless computations and lists, letters and cards, clippings from newspapers — anything that, within the terms and hopes of her life, had seemed valuable or potentially useful or in some way dear.

Among all else she saved were twenty or so letters from Uncle Andrew. Most of these were written on the stationery of hotels in southern states, mostly in South Carolina. All of them show a wish to be a good son, and I have no doubt that this was a wish that he felt genuinely enough when he felt it; I do not think that he felt it all the time. The letters always intend to assure Grandma and Grandpa that he is doing better, or is now all right, or has resolved to lead a cleaner life. He clearly did not like the thought that they were worried about him. And yet there are, even in this small and perhaps selective sheaf that Grandma saved, too many letters of that sort. It is impossible not to suspect that he was trying, as if by incantation, to lay to rest the more obvious consequences of failings that he could not help, or that he did not much want to help. It is almost as if he felt that if he could just stop Grandma and Grandpa, especially Grandma, from worrying, there would be nothing to worry about.

And yet they are troubled letters, and they are troubling. One of them in particular has occupied all alone a large place in my mind since I first read it. It was written a few months after I was born and given his name. According to the letter, he has been "out"—certainly out of a job and perhaps also drunk. But now, he says, "While not making any money am better off than I was, some, and believe in six months will be much better. First want to tell you and ask that you not worry one bit." He is evidently ready to begin work as a salesman for a liquor company. His associates, he says, are "the cleanest bunch of men you ever saw," and they do not drink. But if Grandma wishes, he will try to get another kind of job, which he does not believe would be hard for him to do. He thanks the family for their kindness and consideration of his feelings while he was "out." My mother in particular, he says, has been sweet and thoughtful. They all have shown him such love and affection that he could do nothing that would hurt them or shake their confidence.

And then he writes the sentence — troubled, tender, hopeful, and, as I know, hopeless — that binds me to him closer than my name: "And little Andrew, bless his heart — if for nothing else, I would be a man for him."

11

After I found the letters and read them and put them away again, I assumed that I knew as much about Uncle Andrew as I was ever going to know. I continued to remember him and to think and wonder about him, but I asked no more questions.

And then, thirty years later, after my father died, I found among his papers his file of bills, receipts, and other documents having to do with the settlement of Uncle Andrew's estate. Folded up in that file was a copy of the Hargrave *Weekly Express*, giving an account of the examining trial of Carp Harmon. Why I had not thought before to examine the back issues of the *Weekly Express* I am not sure; I had believed the little I had heard, and perhaps that had satisfied me, but perhaps I also had felt that the truth about Uncle Andrew's death, as long as my father was alive, was his belonging, not mine.

But now, that paper having come to me from my father's very hands, which had folded it and put it away so long ago, I opened it and read the article as eagerly, I think, as I have ever read anything. Much of the article deals with technicalities, but two paragraphs are given to the story of the murder:

"P. R. Gadwell, merchant at Stoneport, testified that Catlett and a group of workers at the lead mine, where buildings were being dismantled, came to the store for lunch and soft drinks. He said Harmon's daughter came in the store and gave her father some change. Gadwell then heard a noise and next saw Catlett getting up after being knocked down by Harmon. Harmon had hit him with an oilcan. He said he heard Catlett apologizing to Harmon, stating he did not know the girl was his daughter. Gadwell said he got Catlett and the other men out of the store but Harmon remained 10 or 15 minutes.

"Jake Branch of near Hargrave, who was assisting Catlett in the dismantling job, said he was 3 or 4 feet from Catlett when the accused hit him with the oilcan. He testified that the group went back to their work and about an hour had elapsed when Harmon suddenly came up to Catlett and said he was going to kill him and pulled a gun. He stated Catlett pleaded that it was 'my mistake' and 'don't shoot me.' Branch said Harmon fired two shots and the workmen rushed Catlett to the hospital.

"R. T. Purlin, 16-year-old stepson of Branch, with the group at the mine, said he yelled to Catlett when he saw Harmon slipping through the weeds but believes Catlett did not hear him."

R. T. Purlin, older than I by six years, had been a hero to Henry and me when we were boys, working and playing together on the Crayton Place, for even at the age of fourteen he was already in body a grown man with an arm like one of Homer's spear throwers, and he never tired of entertaining us with feats of strength. He had a truly clear and generous heart and was never condescending in his friendship to us smaller boys. R. T. was the last living witness to Uncle Andrew's murder. I had not seen him in a long time.

When I called him up and asked if I could come and talk with him, he said, "Yessir! You come right on over here."

The old house that R. T. was living in had no front porch, but a wide back porch ran the length of the ell. Good hounds were chained to their houses under the trees out back.

R. T. came out onto the porch to meet me. "What you been doing all these years?" He talked loudly, like his mother, and had her turns of speech, sounding both like her and like himself.

We went in and sat down at the table in the kitchen where his wife was at work. I complimented his dogs, and we talked a little about coon hunting. R. T. spoke of a tree so full of coons that when their eyes shone back in the beam of his light, the tree looked like a Christmas tree.

We remembered things that had happened on the Crayton Place in the old days. We spoke of his brothers and sisters, whole and half, and of his stepsisters, Jake Branch's daughters by his first wife, and we named and remembered Minnie's six brothers and all the hands who at one time or another had worked for Jake. We spoke of Grandpa Catlett's saddle mare, old Rose, and of Tige and Red, Jake Branch's good team of mules.

Finally I spoke the question I had come to ask: "What happened down there at the lead mine when Carp Harmon shot Uncle Andrew?"

It was hot, R. T. said, when they went back to work in the afternoon, and they were hard at it—all four of them, he and Col Oaks, one of Jake's sons-in-law, Jake himself, and Uncle Andrew. There was a spring of fine cold water down near the road, and after a while Uncle Andrew said, "Jake, let's go get us a drink and leave it with the boys for a while."

The two of them went down to where Uncle Andrew had left his car, just pulled in off the road, to get the top off Uncle Andrew's thermos jug to use as a drinking cup. And then R. T. saw Carp Harmon coming up the road. He ran from one tree or bush to another, trying to stay hidden. When he got near the men at the car, he shot Uncle Andrew, threatened Jake, and ran away down the road again, stopping now and then to look back, R. T. said, "like a sheep-killing dog."

I asked if Uncle Andrew had given some insult to Carp Harmon's daughter when they were down at the store.

R. T. said emphatically, "Nawsir! Andrew never said *nothing* to that girl."

On my way home, I stopped to see my mother. She was sitting in her chair, reading, as she usually is when I come by in the afternoon. And as usual she did not hear me until I rapped loudly on the door of the room where she was sitting. I always expect her to be frightened when I do that, but she never is, being far more reconciled to the unexpected than I am. And so she instructs me.

She looked up, smiled, and said, "Hello! Come in!"

I came in and sat down on the end of the sofa nearest her chair.

"Well, where have you been?"

"I've been to see R. T. Purlin."

"Oh, R. T.!" she said. "What for?"

"To talk," I said.

And then, surprising myself, broaching the issue with her for the first time in my life, I said, "R. T. says that Uncle Andrew didn't say anything sexual at all to Carp Harmon's daughter."

That I could have introduced this subject so abruptly made me aware that we were speaking of Uncle Andrew's death in my father's absence, in the absence of his grief, free of it at last, as I know we both believed that my father was now at last free of it.

"No," my mother said. "He didn't."

The whole business of the sexual insult to the girl, she said, was the defense attorney's lie. Years later, in fact, somebody had told my father that the defense attorney had admitted to the lie. He said that he did not blame my father for disliking him, for he had made the story up.

Thus, suddenly, I was involved in a way I had not expected to be. If the story of the proposition to Carp Harmon's daughter was a lie, then I was implicated in the lie, because for many years I had believed it. But I needed to consider also the possibility that it was *not* true that the defense attorney had lied. If his story was true and our people had falsely denied it, I assumed that this would not have been a deliberate or malicious lie but one that came about simply because those who loved Uncle Andrew, including R. T., could not bear to believe otherwise. And if this belief in Uncle Andrew's innocence was a lie, then I was implicated there also, for I was grateful for whatever comfort it had given to those who had believed it.

❧

Unable now to put it off any longer, I went to the office of the *Weekly Express* and searched out the account of Carp Harmon's trial. According to the article I had already seen, the trial had been set for the September term, but I found that it had been moved to the January term because in September the jurymen had needed to be at home, harvesting their tobacco. In January the jury heard the case and gave their verdict. Carp Harmon received his sentence of two years in the penitentiary. The article in the *Weekly Express* seems meant only to explain the brevity of the sentence. These are the relevant paragraphs:

"During their lunch hour, according to Harmon, Catlett made a remark to Harmon's daughter and Harmon knocked him down. Catlett apologized. Later in the afternoon Harmon went to the scene of work where Catlett and his helpers were and he shot Catlett when Catlett reached for a 2 x 4, following some words between them.

"Harmon testified that he went back to the scene of work to nail a covering over a well. He said Catlett told him to get off the premises along with a remark about his daughter, whom he included in the order to stay away. Harmon said that he fired when Catlett reached for the piece of timber.

"When questioned as to why he had a gun on his person, Harmon said he had been told that someone had run his trotlines."

The jury obviously believed the story of the "remark" to Carp Harmon's daughter — as did the reporter for the *Weekly Express*. If it was a lie, it was the work of a good liar, who could make his story both plausible and consonant with Uncle Andrew's character, which would have been pretty generally known.

The *Weekly Express* writer evidently had believed the story also when it was told six months earlier at the examining trial. What seems significantly different between the two accounts is the appearance in the second of the two-by-four, which was not mentioned in the first.

If the story of the "remark" is true, and if it is true that Carp Harmon's lawyer later admitted that he had told a lie, then the lie may have been this business of the two-by-four, for it is the only reported detail that would have supported an argument of self-defense.

At any rate, I now had learned the basis of the story about the well cover that I had heard when I was a child.

Why, as I got older, did I not ask my father for his version of these events? Now that he is dead, it is easy to wish that I had asked. And yet I know why I did not. I did not want to live again in the great pain I had felt in the old house that night when he had wept so helplessly with Grandma and Grandpa. I did not want to be with him in the presence of that pain where only it and we existed. If I were to speak to his ghost, perhaps I still could not bring myself to ask. When I am a ghost myself, perhaps we will talk of it.

12

If you go toward Stoneport from the high ground instead of along the river, you go at first through a country of excellent broad ridges, farmland greatly respected for its depth and warmth. And then the upland becomes more broken, the ridges narrower, the hollows steeper, the soil thin and rocky. The road to the lead mine turns off one of the ridges and follows a creek bed, usually dry in summer, down into a narrow, wooded hollow. Much of that country is now wooded and has been so for a long time. The farming on those slopes was done in clearings that moved about in place and time as the trees were succeeded by crops, which were succeeded after a short time by a new growth of trees. Now, after its inevitable diminishment by such cropping, the land has been almost entirely given back to the trees.

After it has brought you down nearly to Stoneport on the river, the road passes the site of the old lead mine, which lies off to the right on the far side of the creek. There is still a weedy clearing, originally a hole in the woods to accommodate a hole in the ground. The clearing has remained open because the floor of the hollow has been leveled and covered with tailings from the mine. A squatter has recently lived there in an old bus, which is now abandoned and surrounded by weeds and junk. The main building of the mine, which housed its heavy machinery, was up on the slope. Its foundation, now bare and weathered, straddles the creek, which was used to bear away some of the waste from the extraction of the ore. Behind it, the deep well that Carp Harmon was so anxious to protect is still without a cover; the surface of the water, twenty feet down, is covered with a floating crust of plastic jugs and bottles. Somebody has tried to "improve" the spring of good water down by the road by digging a deep trench into it with a backhoe. The nature of the place seems more insulted by the ordinary acts and artifacts of the present than by the mining of half a century ago.

I went there once with my father when he and Uncle Andrew and the others were in the process of buying the buildings, and I had never been back. I did not even know how to get there until R. T. Purlin went there with me on a hot August afternoon not long after I had hunted up the story of Carp Harmon's trial in the *Weekly Express*.

We pulled off the road, now blacktopped but still just a narrow track coming down through the trees. While we walked over the valley floor and then climbed up over the old foundations into the returning woods, R. T. gave me the story again as the place brought it back to mind.

"Andrew parked his car yonder where you left your truck. Just pulled in off of the road, the way he did every day. Him and Jake went there to get the top off of Andrew's jug on their way to the spring. That fellow stepped out of the bushes must have been right there. Maybe he had stood there a little while, watching them."

He pointed into the air over the foundation of the main building. "Me and Col, we never seen him. We was way up maybe thirty feet in the framework of that building—*big* timbers!—tearing it down. And we heard the shots: *Bam! Bam!*

"I said, 'What the hell was that?'

"And Col said, 'I think that guy has shot Andrew.'

"And down we come."

"Did Uncle Andrew say anything after he was shot?"

"Naw. He went to hurting then. He never said anything."

"And Carp Harmon threatened Jake and ran off?"

"He run right back down the road," R. T. said, and he acted out Carp Harmon's flight, running and then stopping to look back, running and looking back.

"And then you all loaded Uncle Andrew into the car and started for the hospital."

"Yeah."

"And you drove?"

"I was the only one that *could* drive. Jake and Col didn't know how. Andrew had let me drive around a little on the farm. I never had drove on the road. I done pretty good that day till we got up to the top of the lane and onto the blacktop and I started trying to go fast. I had a hard time then to keep in the road. And Andrew was just kicking the car to pieces. We was lucky to make it."

What a ride that must have been for a sixteen-year-old boy who could barely drive, was badly frightened, and who loved the hurt man kicking in pain! In only a few seconds they had been carried from their ordinary work into a moment impossible to be ready for: Uncle Andrew fallen, holding his belly with bloody fingers, Carp Harmon's footsteps going away down the gravel road, nothing now in sight or memory that was quite believable, Uncle Andrew's car sitting there without a driver.

It started to come to me. I began to imagine it, as I knew my father had done, time and again, seeing it as it must have happened and as he could not help seeing it.

And now I too saw them there. I knew how it had been, as if this imagining had suddenly descended to me from my father. I saw them as they lifted Uncle Andrew and got him into the car and as Jake and Col got in, leaving the driver's seat empty.

I heard R. T., not just excited but scared now as well: "Who's going to drive?"

I heard Jake — helpless, angry, bewildered, in a hurry, and yet necessarily resigned: "You are, I reckon."

I saw the black car lurch backward into the road, and then lurch forward, gravel flying from under its wheels as it started up the hill.

And all this happened while I was swimming in the pond, for the moment safe.

❧

R. T. and I loitered around the place a while longer, trying without success to find a rock that R. T. could identify positively as lead ore. He was sure that there had been many such rocks lying around when they had been working down there, but we could find none. Giving up at last, we got into my pickup and started on down toward Stoneport, less than half a mile away.

"And you say Uncle Andrew didn't make a pass at Carp Harmon's daughter?"

"Nawsir. He never," R. T. said. "It was me that girl was talking to.

"I'll show you," he said. We were coming into Stoneport, just a few houses and other buildings scattered around a white weatherboarded church. R. T. showed me the small house where Carp Harmon had lived. He showed me the empty place where fifty years ago had stood the store belonging to P. R. Gadwell. He showed me the place on the roadside opposite where Uncle Andrew had parked his car under the trees.

"I was sitting in the car," R. T. said, "and the girl was leaning against it, talking to me. That fellow could stand in his yard and look right down the road at Andrew's car and see her there. That's how it all got started."

It is a wide street, the view unobstructed from the yard of the house that was Carp Harmon's down to Uncle Andrew's parking spot, a distance of three or four hundred feet. And so R. T.'s version of the story had the plausibility of a true line of sight. It could have happened the way he told it. He could have been himself the bait of a trap that had caught Uncle Andrew.

And yet R. T.'s memory, as I knew by then, was not safe from his imagination. He had told me, on two different days, both that he had and that he had not seen Carp Harmon as he came up the road before the shooting. And on that very day he had told me two versions of his and Col Oaks's hearing the shots; in the first version, R. T. had said, "What the hell was that?" and in the second, Col Oaks had said it. If he had seen the shooting, which he must have done if he had seen Carp Harmon's approach and had tried to warn Uncle Andrew, he apparently had found it too painful to remember. I don't think that these were falsehoods in the usual sense but rather that R. T., in brooding over the story for so many years, had imagined it from shifting points of view, had imagined what he had not seen, had seen what he had not remembered. There is no assurance that he had not imagined also things that had not happened.

If Uncle Andrew had not, in fact, made the "remark" to Carp Harmon's daughter, then why did both P. R. Gadwell and Jake Branch testify that Uncle Andrew apologized to Harmon?

The defense lawyer's story, true or untrue, depended for credibility on the general knowledge of Uncle Andrew's character. I was not the only one who assumed that if he had thought of it, Uncle Andrew would have openly propositioned a girl in a public place. According to that story, as I suppose the jury heard it, a man who lives by impulse invites his own destruction; if he is destroyed as a result of one of his impulsive acts, then a kind of justice has been done. Character is fate, and Carp Harmon was no more than the virtually innocent agent of the appointed fate.

If that story is false, if it *was* R. T. the girl was talking to, then Uncle Andrew's fate had nothing to do with his character and everything to do with chance and the character of Carp Harmon.

But R. T. told me something else that I cannot forget, though perhaps it leads nowhere. He said he had heard that Carp Harmon had been wanting to kill somebody for a long time. "People down there shied him," R. T. said. "He'd been carrying his pistol hid under a rag in the bottom of a ten-quart bucket. He wanted to kill somebody and make a big name for himself. He thought he could kill an outsider and lie his way out of it—which is about what he done."

This story has the standing merely of gossip, but some gossip is true, and Carp Harmon would hardly have been the first of his kind who went about with a hidden gun, looking for somebody to kill. If the piece of gossip *is* true, then the other explanations are not explanations but merely excuses. But a man looking for somebody to kill can presumably find reasons and candidates everywhere, the human race being what it is. If Carp Harmon was in fact such a man, then why did he choose Uncle Andrew, who was not even the only available outsider?

Well, I know too that Carp Harmon was a widower, raising his daughter by himself, undoubtedly afraid for her and afraid for that considerable part of his own self-respect that was at her disposal. And he believed, as he told the court, that somebody was running his trotlines; he was prepared to shoot whoever it was. He was exceptional in none of this—neither in his fear nor in his suspicion nor in his violence.

Nor in his carelessness. Murder, I suppose, is the ultimate carelessness. But Carp Harmon's seems to have been a fearful carelessness, the carelessness of a man who fears that he is small or that he is being held in contempt. And in Uncle Andrew, at least before their violent encounter in

Gadwell's store, he saw a man who must have seemed fearlessly careless, a man completely unabashed, carrying on as he pleased without regard to the possibility that somebody might mind. To a man fearing to be held in contempt, Uncle Andrew would have appeared to be the very holder-in-contempt he had been expecting, whose every gesture identified him as a lifter of skirts and trotlines, a man insufferably sure of himself.

If that is true, then I return again to the thought that Uncle Andrew's character was his fate, and Carp Harmon the agent of it.

But if murder is the ultimate carelessness, it is also the ultimate over-simplifier. It is the paramount act (there are others) by which we reduce a human being to the dimension of one thought. I knew the utterly reckless and fearless, unasking and unanswering Andrew Catlett that Carp Harmon saw. But if Uncle Andrew sometimes possessed a sort of invulnerability of exuberance and regardlessness, he was no longer regardless when he apologized to Carp Harmon. Then he had become pathetic, because, as events would soon prove, it was too late. Carp Harmon cannot have known the quietness and the look by which I knew that Uncle Andrew sometimes bore his life and fate as suffering. Carp Harmon cannot have known, as I know, that for Uncle Andrew there was always a time or a timelessness after (and before) the fact when he wanted to be a better man—if for nothing else, for me.

And all along I have had to wonder what difference I might have made if Uncle Andrew had let me go to Stoneport with him, as I wanted to. Might my presence somehow have unlocked the pattern of the events of that day? Might a small boy, just by being there, have altered the behavior of two reckless men by the tiny shift that might have been needed to change all our lives? Might it be that Uncle Andrew's great mistake was so small a thing as ignoring my advice that I should be taken along? Who can know? Who can know even that the difference, if it had been made, would have been for the better? It might be that if I had gone I would merely have witnessed the shooting. In which case I would not have needed to ask certain questions.

Finally grief has no case to make. All its questions reach beyond the world. And now I am done. The questions remain; the asking is finished. This gathering of fifty-year-old memories, those few brown and brittle pages of newsprint, all those years stand between me and the actual event as irremediably as the end of the world.

Finally you must believe as your heart instructs. If you are a gossip or a cynic or an apostle of realism, you believe the worst you can imagine. If you follow the other way, accepting the bonds of faith and affection, you believe the best you can imagine in the face of the evidence. And so at last, like R. T., I must believe as I imagine and as I therefore choose. I choose not to argue with the story of the "remark" to Carp Harmon's daughter, because it seems both likely and unlikely, and now it makes no difference. I choose not to believe the argument of self-defense; why would even a reckless man with only a two-by-four attack a man with a pistol? I choose to believe that Uncle Andrew said, "Don't shoot me," for it is too plain and sad to be a lie.

And so at last I can imagine it as it might have been.

✻

It is early in the afternoon. The sun is still shining nearly straight down into the tight little valley where Uncle Andrew, Jake Branch, Col Oaks, and R. T. Purlin are dismantling the framework of the main building of the lead mine. The two younger men are at work high up on the heavy timbers, which they are prying loose and letting fall. Uncle Andrew and Jake stand back as the timbers drop, and then move them out of the way and begin pulling out the nails. It is strenuous, dirty, and dangerous work (Uncle Andrew was right not to let me come along). In the small clearing there are stacks of timbers, sorted according to dimension, and piles of corrugated tin. The sun strikes all surfaces with relentless brilliance. Metal objects, including the tools the men are using, if laid down for long, become painful to pick up. There is no breeze; the air is humid, heavy, and still.

Uncle Andrew's sleeves are rolled above his elbows. His arms are shining with sweat and flecked with dirt. His shirt is soaked. And yet he wears his soiled and rumpled clothing and his narrow-brimmed straw hat with a kind of style. He is quick to take part in the talk that comes and goes or to pick up a joke; otherwise his face resumes the expression it has when he is enduring what must be endured. The noontime events down at the store have remained with him. He was knocked down (with an unopened quart can of oil, R. T. said), and he apologized. These facts lie in his belly like something indigestible. What has been done needs undoing, and cannot be undone. As many times before, it is not the present that surprises him but the past, the present slipped away into irrevocability. As many times before, he would like to turn away, find an opening, get out. He feels his own history crowding him, as near to him in that heat as his clinging shirt, as his flesh itself. He feels the weight of the history of flesh. He feels tired. He thinks, "I am already forty-nine years old." He has not drunk since they returned to work, and he is thirsty.

"Jake," he says, "let's go get us a drink, and leave it with the boys for a while."

The two of them put down their tools. They go to the car where Uncle Andrew left his thermos jug, the water in it by then too warm to drink. Off in the shade they can see the spring flowing out beneath its mossy ledge.

And then Carp Harmon steps from behind the trees, already close, and he has a pistol in his hand. Two men, both drawn to that giddy edge where people do what they think of doing, have come face-to-face, and one holds a pistol, and one does not.

"I'm going to kill you," Carp Harmon says, and Uncle Andrew knows he means it.

This, I imagine, was his second direct confrontation with his fate, the first having occurred in the road ditch on the night before his wedding. And I imagine that in this latter moment he knew clearly at last what he was: a man dearly beloved, in spite of his faults.

"Don't shoot me," he says. He is praying, not to Carp Harmon, but to another possibility, his own sudden vision of what he means to the rest of us — of what we all had meant and the much more that we might have meant to one another.

"Don't shoot me."

And Carp Harmon fires forever his two shots.

13

Except for his silent whirl with Mrs. Partlet that afternoon in Minnie Branch's kitchen, I never saw Uncle Andrew dance, but prompted by so many who did see and who remembered, I have often imagined him dancing.

He went into the music, I imagine, alert and aware and yet abandoned, as one might go running into the dark. Invested with the power that women granted him, he would be wholly given over to the music, almost gravely submitted to that which moved him, and yet elated, in reckless exuberance carried away.

I imagine a ballroom in some hotel — in Lexington or Louisville, or Columbia or Charleston — a large room dimly lit, a band on a dais at one end. The room smells of flowers, perfume, tobacco smoke. There is loud talking and laughter, Uncle Andrew in the thick of it, a little drunk. There is a sort of aura of careless delight about him, a suppressed extravagance of physical elation, as though he might at any moment do something that will draw the attention of the whole room to him. He seems himself to be unaware of this.

He is aware of the woman sitting beside him. (Who is she? She is, let us say, Aphrodite herself, for the while. Custom cannot stale her infinite variety.) For the while his being is directed toward her like the beam of a lamp, and she knows it. She casts back his light, granting him love — as I did, as we all did, because he had the power of attracting it; not ever asking for it, he called it forth.

The band members shift in their seats, take up their instruments, and begin another song. They play "Don't Get Around Much Anymore," a song elegant and inconsolable. (It may have come too late for him to have danced to it, but it is the one song I can remember hearing him sing, and so I imagine him dancing to it.) He reaches out without a word; the woman gives him her hand. They rise and walk onto the floor, dancing even before they dance. They step into the music. The woman's weight on his arm, given to him, he forgets his feet. The two of them ask and answer one another, motion for motion. He holds her with an assurance that is almost forgetfulness, and yet is entirely attentive to her and to the song that moves them:

> *Darling I guess*
> *My mind's more at ease*
> *But nevertheless*
> *Why stir up memories*
>
> *Been invited on dates*
> *Might have gone but what for*
> *Awf'lly diff'rent without you*
> *Don't get around much anymore.*

A trumpet solo sways, gleaming, in the air. Under it the man and woman turn and soar. The woman rests upon his arm, leaning back, at one with him in their now weightless flight. The little while it lasts, he does not know where he is.

14

One day maybe forty years ago my father told Elton Penn, "I almost did something once that I would have been awfully sorry for."

Elton told Henry and me not long afterward. We had been at work and were resting, as it happened, in the shade of some locust trees beside the tobacco barn that had been built of our share of the materials salvaged from the lead mine. Henry and I were grown boys then, eligible to be told things that Elton found it lonely to know by himself.

"I wonder what he meant," Elton said. "I couldn't ask him."

The two of them had been in my father's car, driving through the fields, looking at the condition of everything and talking, as they often did. My father, for some reason, reached over and opened the glove compartment. When he did so, Elton saw a small nickel-plated .32 revolver lying among the papers and other things my father kept there.

"What are you carrying that for, Wheeler?" Elton asked.

I no longer remember the reason. Probably he was on the lookout for stray dogs. He had sheep in those days, and dogs were always a worry.

Elton asked him if he had bought the pistol in fear that he might need to defend himself. We all knew that my father had once defended a man in a murder trial, at the end of which the acquitted defendant had been shot and killed by the victim's brother. Elton wanted to hear about that. But my father only shook his head and said that once he had almost done something he would have been sorry for.

Sitting under the locusts, we tried to think what it might have been. We decided, with the barn there to remind us, that it must have had something to do with Carp Harmon, though we did not know for sure.

Of course, we did not know at all. I don't remember that any of us ever brought up the subject again, though we were all much interested in my father and we talked about him interminably.

He fascinated us, I think, because he was so completely alive and passionate and intelligent, so precisely intent upon the things he loved, so eager to get work done, so fiercely demanding of us, and yet so tender toward us. We would be angry at him often enough, and yet he delighted us, and we were proud of him. Elton loved to mimic my father's way of driving up in his car in a hurry, rolling the window down, patting the accelerator with his foot while he talked to you, and then — bzzzt! — taking off again, sometimes in the midst of your answer to what he had just asked you. He could use the telephone the same way, hanging up the instant he found out what he had called to learn, leaving you talking to the dead receiver. But sometimes when you were out at work he would seem just to ease up out of nowhere; you would look up and there he would be, sitting in the car, watching you and smiling, glad to have found you, glad to be there with you. Wonderful conversations sometimes happened at those times.

One day in the early spring Elton was disking ground a long way from the house. The day turned cold, and he had not worn enough clothes. Gradually the chill sank into him until his bones ached. And then, as he came to the end of one of his rounds, he saw my father driving up. Elton left the tractor and got into the car. My father turned up the heater and the two of them sat there and talked of the coming year while Elton quit shivering and got warm. Finally, having only a little left to do, Elton returned to the tractor and my father went on wherever he was going.

In such wanderings and encounters, my father enacted his belonging to his country and his people. He could be as peremptory and harsh as a saw — we younger ones all had felt his edge — but he knew how to be a friend. One night when he was old, he named over to me all those of the dead who had been his friends. He said, "If they are there, Paradise is Paradise indeed."

He had a horseman's back, like his father, and would often sit on a chair as if it were a stool. He was wide awake and on watch, as if he expected a fly ball to be hit to him at any moment. He rarely loitered or ambled. Until he began to fail, when he was well into his eighties, he moved with great energy, a certain lightness, and the resolution sometimes of a natural force.

Even his gaiety was resolute. Or his gaiety came of a sort of freedom within his resolution. He was determined to do what he had to do; he would look for no escape; he was free. I always loved to watch him dress for the office, for often at that time he would be in a high good humor, dancing as he buttoned his shirt and knotted his tie, sometimes already wearing his hat before he put on his pants. He had things he wanted to do, and he could hardly wait.

I sat many a time, waiting for him, in the outer office where Miss Julia sat, typing, at her desk. I would know he was coming when I heard the street door open suddenly and almost in the same moment slam shut, rattling the glass, and then I would hear his footsteps light and rapid on the stairs, for characteristically he would be running. At the top, there would be two hard footfalls to check his speed, and he would hit the door, turning the knob, and the door would open as by the force of an explosion in the hallway, admitting my father, who would say all in one sentence: "Hello Andy Miss Julia what did we do with that Buttermore file?"

It would be the same when he came home: swift footfalls on the porch steps, three long strides across the porch followed by the implosion of the door — and there would be my father going full tilt to hang up his hat.

One day not long after Carp Harmon had been released from the penitentiary, my mother heard that pattern of sounds when she should not have heard it: in the middle of the morning. Nobody but my father came into the house that way, and she went to see what had brought him home. All this she told me after he was dead.

When she came into the front of the house, he was taking that little nickel-plated pistol from the top of the corner cupboard in the dining room.

"What are you doing?" she said.

It measures the strength of his love for her that he answered her straight. He said that he had seen Carp Harmon in town, and he was going to kill him.

I know well the look that anger put into my father's eyes; I can guess the size of the job my mother had on her hands.

She put herself in his way. She told him that killing Carp Harmon would not bring Uncle Andrew back. She told him he had more to think about than just Uncle Andrew. Or just himself. He had to think of his children, who would have to live with what he did.

He had to think of her.

It took her a long time, but she talked him out of it. He put the gun away.

She had spoken the simple truth: He could not bring Uncle Andrew back; he could not make justice by his own hand, according to his own will. She knew he was almost defeated, fallen under the weight of mortality and affliction and his own inclination toward the evil that afflicted him; he was nearly lost. And she called him back to his life and to us.

He told her one day that now he had nothing to live for.

"And then," she told me, "I let him have it. I felt for him as much as one human ever felt for another, but I let him have it. And it *did good!*"

In that time of grief and discouragement and defeat—it comes clear to me now—all that my father was and would ever be depended on my mother. I can see how near he came to turning loose all that he held together, and how, in holding it together, with my mother's help, he preserved the possibility of our life here; he quieted himself, lived, stayed on, bore what he had to bear. With my mother's help, he kept alive in his life our lives as they would be.

15

In the summer that I turned ten, the summer of Uncle Andrew's death, all the tobacco and corn on the Crayton Place was grown in the same field in the middle of the farm. The field was divided in two by a road, just a dirt track, by which we went from the gate on one side to the gate on the other. To the left of the road, going back, was a long, broad ridge, sloping gently to the fences on either side. To the right of the road and on the far side of the ridge, the slope was broken by hollows and was somewhat steeper. The field was beautifully laid out, so that all the rows followed the contours of the ridge. This was particularly noticeable in that far right-hand corner where the plowlands were smaller and were divided by grassed drains. The design of the field would have been my father's work: a human form laid lovingly upon the natural conformation of the place.

There came a morning when I stood in the dust of the road with a hoe in my hands, looking at the field, and was overcome by sudden comprehension of what was happening there. The corn was a little above knee-high, the tobacco plants about the size of a man's hat, both crops green and flourishing. R. T. and I were hoeing the tobacco. I could see Jake Branch plowing corn with a riding cultivator drawn by a good pair of black, white-nosed mules named Jack and Pete. Somewhere beyond the ridgetop, Col Oaks was plowing tobacco with a single mule, old Red, and a walking plow. The air smelled of vegetation and stirred earth. Beside me, R. T. was filing his hoe. Standing there in the brilliance with my ears sticking out under the brim of my straw hat and my mouth probably hanging open (somebody was always telling me, "Shut your mouth, Andy!"), I saw how beautiful the field was, how beautiful our work was. And it came to me all in a feeling how everything fitted together, the place and ourselves and the animals and the tools, and how the sky held us. I saw how sweetly we were enabled by the land and the animals and our few simple tools.

My moment of vision cannot have lasted long. It ended, I imagine, when R. T. finished sharpening his hoe and nudged me with the file and handed it to me. It was a powerful moment, a powerful vision nonetheless. I have lived under its influence ever since.

Its immediate result was that I became frantic to own a mule. I saw how, owning a mule, a boy could become a man, an economic entity, dignified and self-sustaining, capable of lovely work. I fixed my mind on Pete, who was a little the tallest and a little the most stylish of the pair Jake Branch was working that day in the corn rows. My conversations with Uncle Andrew were all dominated by my obsessive importunings and proposals for the purchase of the mule. I wanted to buy him on credit, giving Uncle Andrew and my father my note for the full amount, and pay for him by my work—which, given my irregular employment at a quarter a day, would have taken quite a while.

It was a boy's dream, sufficiently absurd, and yet the passion that attached to it I am still inclined to respect, for I still feel it. But Uncle Andrew thought my obsession was funny, when he did not think it a nuisance. This was my first inkling that, as much as I wanted to be like him, we were not alike. It was not a difference that I rationalized or made much of, but I remember that it troubled me; something in the way I was had set me apart from him, and I could not help but feel it. Though I know more fully now than then how much I loved him, and though I love him still, that is still a memory that troubles me.

After his death, anyhow, I went on to teachers who were more exacting: to Elton Penn, for one, and through Elton, to my father. Elton, whose father had died when Elton was only a little boy, had made himself a student to my grandfather Catlett and to my father. My father thus spoke to me through Elton before I learned to listen to him in his own right. And so from the influence of Uncle Andrew I came at last under the influence of my father, as perhaps I was destined to do from the first.

Elton and my father were alike in their love for farming and for work well done. They loved the application of intelligence to problems. They saw visions of things that could be done, and they drew great excitement both from the visions themselves and from their practical results. I loved those qualities in them, and longed to find or make the same qualities in myself.

My father could be gentle to the point of tenderness, but he was not invariably so. In certain moods, he had a way of landing on you like a hawk on a rabbit. He could be wondrously impatient; whatever needed doing he wanted already done by the time he thought of it, which would have been going some. Or he could be fiercely put out because you did not already know whatever he was trying to teach you. Sometimes this amused Elton—he enjoyed mimicking my father in such moods—but he suffered from it too, and so I could expect a certain amount of sympathy from him.

One day when I was angry at my father and needed somebody to complain to, I found Elton out by his garden, sharpening bean poles. He was kneeling on the ground in front of a small chopping block. He would take a pole from the pile on his left, stand it on the block, point it with three or four light licks of his hatchet, and lay it in the pile on his right. I sat down, not offering to help, and began my complaint. Elton listened to me, working steadily with his head down. For a long time he said nothing.

Finally he said, "Well, you've got responsibilities, you know, that he's trying to get you ready for."

I had known for a while what my answer to that would be, and I liked the way it was going to sound: "My responsibilities can go to hell."

Elton stopped with the hatchet still in the air and looked at me with a look that seemed to originate somewhere way back in his head. He started to grin.

He said, "You don't know tumblebug language, do you?"

"No," I said.

He was wearing a leather glove on his right hand and he pulled it off. He held up two fingers in a V to represent the tumblebug's feelers. He wiggled the right-hand finger: "Roll it to the right!" He wiggled the left-hand finger: "Roll it to the left!" He wiggled both fingers: "Stop that shit!"

He wiggled both fingers at me with that look in his eyes and grinned, and the grin kept getting bigger.

I did not stop it that day, of course, for I had a long way still to go to be a grown man; sometimes I see that I have not altogether stopped it yet. But I had received the sign I was looking for.

16

I remember a later day — I was in college by then — when I went to my father's office to tell him of a certain very rough hill farm I wanted to buy in partnership with Elton Penn. It was a cool, bright day at the end of summer, the tobacco crop was in the barn, and Elton and I had been on the back of his place, disking the harvested field and drilling it in wheat.

We finished early in the afternoon, and dipped the last of the unplanted seed out of the drill. The Markman Place, adjoining Elton's at the back, had been put up for sale, and we stood leaning on the drill box in the satisfaction of the field replanted and safe for the winter, wondering who the buyer would be. The farm had been owned by an old couple, like many others, whose children had grown up and scattered to the towns. The husband had died on the place a good many years ago, and then, that spring, the wife had died at a nursing home down at Hargrave. Who the new owner would be was a mystery that troubled Elton, for it was unlikely that anybody would buy such a farm — small and off the road and now run down — as a place to live.

He stood silently looking over the fence a moment, and then he said, "Let's go over there and look at it."

And so we did. We climbed over the fence and started across a weedy field toward the house and outbuildings. Beyond the line fence the ridges grew narrower and dropped away toward the wooded hollows. Since the onset of Amster Markman's last illness, the farm had been cropped by a neighbor and otherwise unused. Briars and sumacs and young sassafras trees had begun to colonize in patches the pasture we were walking through.

We jumped a rabbit, and Elton mimed a shot, snapping an imaginary gun to his shoulder. I knew his mood. He was feeling free and excited; the most anxious stage of the year's work was behind him.

We went first to the house and walked around it, through the overgrown yard, to the front porch. We had in mind to look in through the windows — at least I did — but when we had climbed the steps we went no further. Miss Gladys Markman's ruffled curtains were still hanging in the windows. The porch swing still swung from its rusty hooks.

At the edge of the porch we stood and looked out past the sugar maple in the yard and over the tops of the trees on the bluff into the Bird's Branch valley. You could not help but imagine Gladys and Amster Markman, old and alone, sitting there in the cool of the evening.

"It's a fine place for a house," Elton said.

"It is," I said, moved by possibility.

"And it's a good house, too," Elton said. "It's been kept up. Nothing wrong with it at all." He looked at me and grinned, knowing that I had a girl I was serious about down at Hargrave.

We went on around the other side of the house and drew a drink from the well by the kitchen door. Elton stood with his hand still on the pump handle, looking at the weed-covered garden plot and the lots out by the barns. "Nobody going out to milk here *this* evening," he said.

The old tobacco barn was twisted and leaning as though about to collapse under the weight of its roof. The small feed barn was still straight, square, level, and plumb; we went in through the half-open door. The field we had walked across had been unscarred beneath the weed growth, and now we saw that Amster Markman had planted flagstones edge-up beneath the stall partitions and thus kept the manure from rotting the wood.

"He was a good farmer," Elton said. "He had that name."

There were stalls for four horses on one side of the driveway. On the other side there was a little feed room and two large pens, one with tie chains and troughs for five cows. A set of old harness still hung from pegs in front of two of the stalls. All the doors had neat wooden latches. There was still hay in the loft.

When we stepped out again into the daylight, Elton said, "Let's you and me buy this old place and set it to rights."

He was watching me, grinning again, to see how the thought would hit me. Remembering it now, I cannot be sure how serious he was. It was at least a thought that he could not resist thinking. And he was grinning, I suppose, because he knew that I could not resist it either.

"But how would I get the money?" I said.

"I don't know." He was still looking at me, grinning, poking in his shirt pocket for his cigarettes. "Maybe Wheeler would help you. You ought to ask him."

The possibility then seemed to descend upon us and envelop us, like a sudden change of weather. It changed everything: our minds, the day, the place.

We went into the careening tobacco barn.

"The framing and innards are all sound," Elton said. "It could be straightened up."

We spent a quarter of an hour dreaming aloud of what could be done. And then we walked in the other ridgetop fields, down into the woods, and back up by the lane that went out to the road.

"Here's a place where a young fellow could get started and go on," Elton said.

I knew it was. The thought of it had already gone all through me. It aches in me yet, though the Markman Place never became a real farm again and the house was vandalized and finally burned by hunters.

By the time we crossed the line fence again we knew the layout of the place, and we had thought of a way to farm it.

※

And so, late that afternoon, I climbed up the sounding well of my father's office stairs, the noises of the street shut out behind me so that I rose up within the sound of my own steps. At the top of the stairs I took the two further steps to the office door and opened it into the waiting room, now empty, where Miss Julia Vye's typewriter sat beneath its gray cover. The room was full of the level-lying late sunlight that entered through the back windows. I shut the door quietly and took another couple of steps to see if my father was at his desk.

He had already swiveled his chair around. He was smiling. He said, "Come in, Andy."

He was in one of his beautiful times. I knew of the times when he would quietly enter the shade where his cattle were resting, and sit down. I knew too that he loved the seldom-occurring times late in the afternoons when he sat on at his desk after the office had emptied, when he could be as quiet as the room, ordering his thoughts. It was a time when time seemed to have stopped and his work itself was at rest.

Sometimes when I interrupted him at work in the press of a day's events, he could be short enough, but now he welcomed me into his ease.

"Sit down. I'm glad to see you."

He positioned a chair for me and I sat down. He laid his writing pad on top of one of the neat stacks of books and papers on his desk. He screwed the top back onto his fountain pen, took off his glasses and rubbed his eyes, and then he looked at me.

"What have you got on your mind?"

I told him. Though I guessed that he already knew the Markman Place, I described it to him as Elton and I had seen it, walking over it. I told him the possibilities we had seen.

My father's attention, when he freely turned it to you, was a benevolent atmosphere. His hearing was the native element of my tale. He knew what I had seen; he had imagined such restorations as I had imagined; he had felt my excitement and my longing. The possibility I was trying to find voice for—an old place renewed and carried on—had kept him a farmer, though he was also a lawyer; it had sent him into endless struggles. Now, having lived to the age he was then and past it, and thinking of my own children, I know how stirred he was, listening to me, for he was hearing his own passion uttered to him by his son.

And yet he talked me out of it.

"Wait," he said. "You've got more directions in you than you know."

He wanted me to be free for a while longer. Perhaps he felt free to keep me free because he saw that I was already securely bound; my wish of that day would not leave me, though I had yet to drift far from it and return. In talking me out of my hope, he accorded it a gentleness that enabled me to keep it always.

17

Now that I have told virtually all I know of the story of Uncle Andrew and of his death and how we fared afterward, I see that I must return to my old question — What manner of man was he? — and make peace with it, for I am by no means certain of the answer. A story, I see, is not a life. A story must follow a line; the telling must begin and end. A life, on the contrary, would be impossible to fix in time, for it does not begin within itself, and it does not end.

Within limits we can know. Within somewhat wider limits we can imagine. We can extend compassion to the limit of imagination. We can love, it seems, beyond imagining. But how little we can understand!

Whatever he was, Uncle Andrew was more than I know. In drawing him toward me again after so long a time, I seem to have summoned, not into view or into thought, but just within the outmost reach of love, Uncle Andrew in the plenitude of his being — the man he would have been for my sake, and for love of us all, had he been capable. In recalling him as I knew him in mortal time, I have felt his presence as a living soul.

However we may miss and mourn the dead, we really give little deference to death. "Death," a friend of mine said as he approached it himself, "is a convention . . . not binding upon anyone but the keepers of graveyard records." The dead remain in thought as much alive as they ever were, and yet increased in stature and grown remarkably near. The older I have got and the better acquainted among the dead, the plainer it has become to me that I live in the company of immortals.

❦

One by one, the sharers in this mortal damage have borne its burden out of the present world: Uncle Andrew, Grandpa Catlett, Grandma, Momma-pie, Aunt Judith, my father, and many more. At times perhaps I could wish them merely oblivious, and the whole groaning and travailing world at rest in their oblivion. But how can I deny that in my belief they are risen?

I imagine the dead waking, dazed, into a shadowless light in which they know themselves altogether for the first time. It is a light that is merciless until they can accept its mercy; by it they are at once condemned and redeemed. It is Hell until it is Heaven. Seeing themselves in that light, if they are willing, they see how far they have failed the only justice of loving one another; it punishes them by their own judgment. And yet, in suffering that light's awful clarity, in seeing themselves within it, they see its forgiveness and its beauty, and are consoled. In it they are loved completely, even as they have been, and so are changed into what they could not have been but what, if they could have imagined it, they would have wished to be.

That light can come into this world only as love, and love can enter only by suffering. Not enough light has ever reached us here among the shadows, and yet I think it has never been entirely absent.

Remembering, I suppose, the best days of my childhood, I used to think I wanted most of all to be happy — by which I meant to be here and to be undistracted. If I were here and undistracted, I thought, I would be at home.

But now I have been here a fair amount of time, and slowly I have learned that my true home is not just this place but is also that company of immortals with whom I have lived here day by day. I live in their love, and I know something of the cost. Sometimes in the darkness of my own shadow I know that I could not see at all were it not for this old injury of love and grief, this little flickering lamp that I have watched beside for all these years.

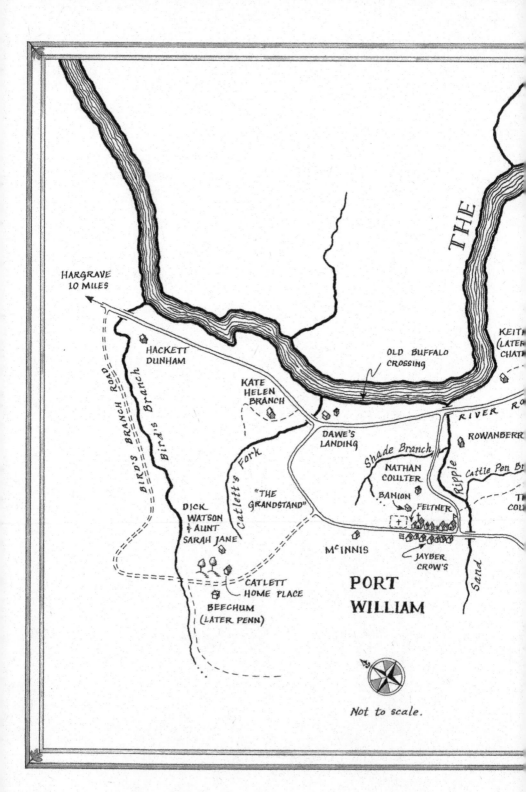

HARGRAVE
10 MILES

HACKETT
DUNHAM

KATE
HELEN
BRANCH

OLD BUFFALO
CROSSING

THE

KEITH
(LATER
CHATH

RIVER RO

ROWANBERR

DAWE'S
LANDING

Shade Branch

Cattle Pen Br

NATHAN
COULTER

BANION

FELTNER

"THE
GRANDSTAND"

Ripple

TH
COLL

DICK
WATSON
& AUNT
SARAH JANE

McINNIS

JAYBER
CROW'S

Sand

CATLETT
HOME PLACE

PORT

BEECHUM
(LATER PENN)

WILLIAM

Not to scale.

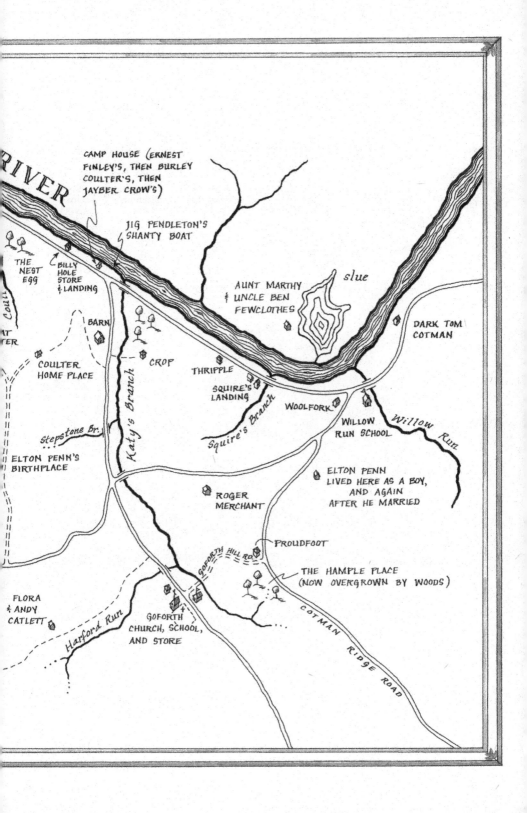

RIVER

CAMP HOUSE (ERNEST
FINLEY'S, THEN BURLEY
COULTER'S, THEN
JAYBER CROW'S)

JIG PENDLETON'S
SHANTY BOAT

THE
NEST
EGG

BILLY
HOLE
STORE
& LANDING

Coulter

AT
TER

BARN

COULTER
HOME PLACE

Stepstone Br.

ELTON PENN'S
BIRTHPLACE

Katy's Branch

CROP

THRIPPLE

SQUIRE'S
LANDING

Squire's Branch

ROGER
MERCHANT

slue

AUNT MARTHY
& UNCLE BEN
FEWCLOTHES

DARK TOM
COTMAN

WOOLFORK

WILLOW
RUN SCHOOL

Willow Run

ELTON PENN
LIVED HERE AS A BOY,
AND AGAIN
AFTER HE MARRIED

PROUDFOOT

GOFORTH HILL RD.

THE HAMPLE PLACE
(NOW OVERGROWN BY WOODS)

FLORA
& ANDY
CATLETT

Harford Run

GOFORTH
CHURCH, SCHOOL,
AND STORE

COTMAN
RIDGE
ROAD

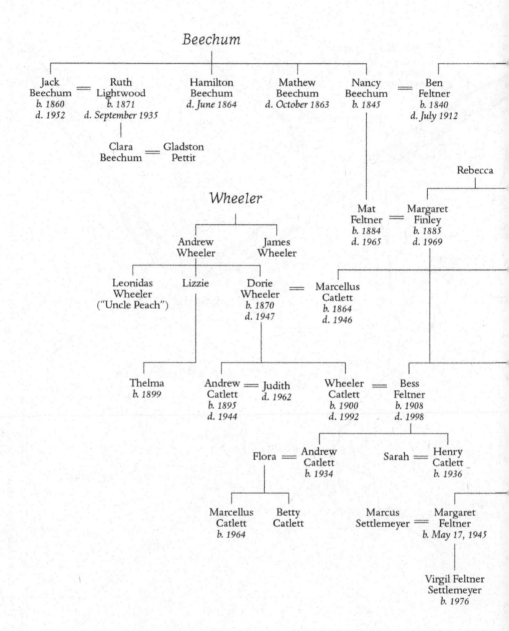

Beechum

Jack Beechum *b. 1860 d. 1952* ══ Ruth Lightwood *b. 1871 d. September 1935*

Hamilton Beechum *d. June 1864*

Mathew Beechum *d. October 1863*

Nancy Beechum *b. 1845* ══ Ben Feltner *b. 1840 d. July 1912*

Clara Beechum ══ Gladston Pettit

Rebecca

Wheeler

Andrew Wheeler

James Wheeler

Mat Feltner *b. 1884 d. 1965* ══ Margaret Finley *b. 1885 d. 1969*

Leonidas Wheeler ("Uncle Peach")

Lizzie

Dorie Wheeler *b. 1870 d. 1947* ══ Marcellus Catlett *b. 1864 d. 1946*

Thelma *b. 1899*

Andrew Catlett *b. 1895 d. 1944* ══ Judith *d. 1962*

Wheeler Catlett *b. 1900 d. 1992* ══ Bess Feltner *b. 1908 d. 1998*

Flora ══ Andrew Catlett *b. 1934*

Sarah ══ Henry Catlett *b. 1936*

Marcellus Catlett *b. 1964*

Betty Catlett

Marcus Settlemeyer ══ Margaret Feltner *b. May 17, 1945*

Virgil Feltner Settlemeyer *b. 1976*

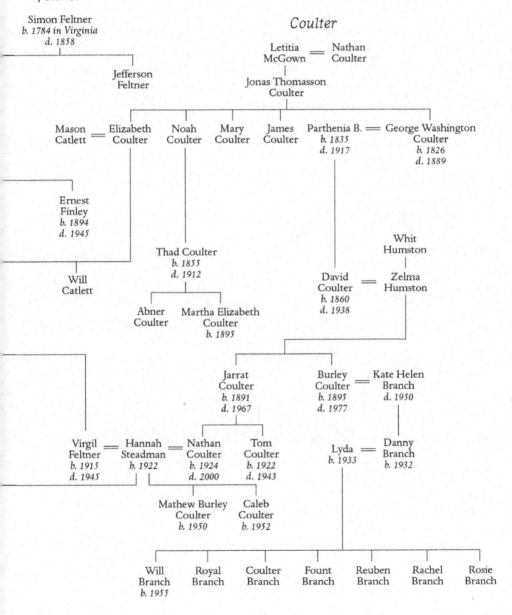

Feltner

Simon Feltner
b. 1784 in Virginia
d. 1858

Jefferson
Feltner

Coulter

Letitia
McGown ═══ Nathan
Coulter

Jonas Thomasson
Coulter

Mason
Catlett ═══ Elizabeth
Coulter   Noah
Coulter   Mary
Coulter   James
Coulter   Parthenia B.
b. 1835
d. 1917 ═══ George Washington
Coulter
b. 1826
d. 1889

Ernest
Finley
b. 1894
d. 1945

Will
Catlett

Thad Coulter
b. 1855
d. 1912

Whit
Humston

Abner
Coulter   Martha Elizabeth
Coulter
b. 1895

David
Coulter
b. 1860
d. 1938 ═══ Zelma
Humston

Jarrat
Coulter
b. 1891
d. 1967

Burley
Coulter
b. 1895
d. 1977 ═══ Kate Helen
Branch
d. 1950

Virgil
Feltner
b. 1915
d. 1945 ═══ Hannah
Steadman
b. 1922 ═══ Nathan
Coulter
b. 1924
d. 2000   Tom
Coulter
b. 1922
d. 1943

Lyda
b. 1933 ═══ Danny
Branch
b. 1932

Mathew Burley
Coulter
b. 1950   Caleb
Coulter
b. 1952

Will
Branch
b. 1955   Royal
Branch   Coulter
Branch   Fount
Branch   Reuben
Branch   Rachel
Branch   Rosie
Branch